2

ISLANDS

A Collection of Short Stories

David Rees

Knights
Press

Stamford, Connecticut

Designed by Able Reproductions, copyright © 1984
Published by Knights Press, P.O. Box 454, Pound Ridge, NY 10576

Library of Congress Cataloging in Publication Data

Rees, David.
  Islands.
  1. Homosexuality—Fiction. I. Title.
PR6068.E36818   823'.914   84-19408
ISBN 0-915175-06-1 (pbk.)

Printed in the United States of America

For Hugh Brogan

No man is an island entire of itself; every man is a piece of the continent, a part of the main.

—John Donne, *Devotions*

CONTENTS

Cliff

Rain drumming on the tent roof woke me. It was so dark that not even the faintest outlines could be seen; only Gary's deep-sleep breathing just by me and those fairy drumsticks pattering proved that anything still existed. I turned over. Tightness in my bladder had woken me, but I was snug in the warm sleeping bag; I was not going to get up. It was daft; why did it have to protest in the early hours? Last night's beer and last night's sex, I imagine. Gary and I had been lovers for a month: we couldn't leave each other's bodies alone. It usually ended up with him screwing me, and that bothered me a little. I wanted, much of the time, to be inside him. To prove my maleness? I don't know. I unpeeled myself from the sleeping bag and groped for the flaps. After the tent's sleepy heat the cold of the ground shocked me into full consciousness; my feet squelched in the wet mud and the rain on my warm naked skin was like needles.

Back in the tent I curled up round Gary in the hot double sleeping bag: it was good to be zipped in, much more satisfying than being in a bed with sheets. Disturbed by my movements, he muttered in his sleep, and licked his lips several times. I stroked his arms, his thighs.

In the morning I was first to wake, and I crept out, leaving Gary to snore. It had stopped raining, but the clouds were low down over the hills, grey and smoky, not a break in them. The scree that scarred the nearby hillside glistened after the rain, the boulders at its foot wet and sharp. They looked as if they had only rolled to rest a moment ago.

"Lousy weather," Gary said, emerging.

"What are you going to do this morning?"

He looked up at the clouds, then dabbled gingerly at the ground with one foot. "Maybe right for a spot of fishing," he said. "Yes, I think I'll go fishing." He looked towards the stream, still vague in the mist, down among the jumble of rocks and pebbles.

"I think I'll take a walk down to the sea and try the cliff," I said.

"What . . . climbing?"

"Why not?"

"Is it safe?"

I shrugged. "I don't know. Seemed all right yesterday evening."

"So you've had a look. I might have guessed. What about breakfast? Bread and marmalade? Tea?" He went back to the tent. "Tell you what," he said, rummaging around in his pack for a knife, "if you're not back in reasonable time, I'll come down after you and look for your remains. Your bits and pieces."

The stream sucked and gurgled along beside me, lapping round blocks of granite that its winter force had dragged down from the hills. The grass stopped half a mile from the beach and I was walking on bare earth. There was a long cleft up the hill on the far side of the stream as if ice had once burst the walls of the land apart and released the shower of stones that now formed the wide scree beneath it. There was a breeze, and the clouds above began to shift, revealing other layers of grey and brown cloud that frothed in slow motion in patterns which dispersed and reformed almost at once into new patterns. It was cold; the cliffs, I had reckoned, would be hot work, so I was wearing only shorts, sweater and sneakers.

The tide was coming in, slowly rubbing out the lines of rock, infiltrating the gaps between fingers of seaweed. Bright ribbons of weed, amber and rust, and shell-fish in pools – limpets and winkles – softened the hard grey shapes of the beach. For the first time that day I noticed the birds: a solitary guillemot, wings cutting the air like scissor blades; then a little colony of gulls, dazzling white feathers on a ledge patiently watching the incoming sea; and out beyond the waves small diving birds, brown and in pairs, disappearing then bobbing up yards away, busy with activity. Shattered rocks marked the limit of this beach; they were knotty pointing fingers, threatening vengeance at the clouds, and lines of dogs' teeth suggesting a petrified monster beneath the sea. The cliff I was going to climb was the end of the hill that formed one side of the valley down which I had just walked. The vertical drop showed a cross-section of the hill's inside, an X-ray of its bones and nerves. The hill was a shoulder heaving up through the earth: it had been frozen in its upward thrust centuries ago in pre-history, and whatever sea or earthquake or glacier had formed it had also torn half the limb away, and ripped it into thousands of fragments which were now the wilderness of boulders scattered about the beach at its base.

I started. The route, or at least a bit of it, had been worked out in my mind's eye yesterday when I came down for a swim. I was alone then as now – Gary had stayed by the fire cooking lamb chops – and it seemed that no other human had ever swum there. Me, the scenery, nothing else. I had noticed then the diagonal fracture in the rock: it was a line, about two feet wide, that rose up half-way, a hundred and fifty feet perhaps.

The fault did not rise as evenly as I had thought. In places it became almost level, making little platforms on which birds had nested earlier in the year. I paused on the third platform, looking down at the sea slowly rising over the rocks. When I started again, my sneakers slipped. My right leg cracked down hard on the ledge, and when the moment of terror was over, I found myself gripping a protruding turret of stone. I looked down through my legs, and there was nothing but air between me and the spiked rocks on the beach.

I pulled myself upright. The fall had merely grazed the skin, but there were voices advising me to return to sea level while there was still time. I went on, up. There was no ignoring the sheer drop on my right, but as I heaved and kicked my way up the next vertical section, I looked only at my hands and arms and knees and the patches of cliff-face they were negotiating. My fingertips fumbled for the edge of stone that would hold, although the sensitive skin under the nails objected to the rough earth and chips pressed into it. This voice, too, had to be silenced. Then the biceps pulled, and the bag of bones and breath that was me was dragged a few inches higher; knees and leg muscles pressed into a chink, and the biceps' gain was made safe. Up went a leg as high as it could stretch, so that the toe-cap of the sneaker could feel the safety of the cranny; another heave of the biceps and I was lying on the next, almost flat, step. Little springs of perspiration trickled down into my eyes, and I was glad now I was wearing only sweater and shorts. I thought of arms dissected, as in a biology book diagram, and the labeled cross-section: muscle from humerus to scapula, biceps (flexes arms), triceps (extends arms), ulna, muscles which flex wrist and fingers, ligaments holding carpals. That was all it was, a system of levers, pulleys, hinges, and joints for dragging and pulling, with nerves to register the dissatisfied urges: eat, drink, sleep, fuck, save me. Yet the bicep, knotted into its tight ball, was one of the signs of strength, of being a man, no longer the sleek and satin upper arm of a boy. Some obscure urge always said that it must be better to be a man than a boy, and the stronger and more powerful the signs of a man the better. It was only because I wanted to prove I was less weedy than other people: it was stupid climbing up cliffs just to test myself. Nevertheless, it had to be done.

I stopped again. It was not so worrying now, looking at the sea. The sharp claws down there had merged into their surroundings; they were not half so fierce this far away. I dangled my legs over the edge and deliberately looked down, humming a tune. "I am what I am, and what I am needs no excuses . . . " The pools the sea had not yet reached were mirrors without reflections; light shone from them, but the breeze ruffled their surfaces, spoiling the upturned clouds I should see there. The white edges of waves fretted the rocks, and occasionally sent up a petulant column of spray. The sound was gentle and soothing, a wordless dirge for several voices. Above, the clouds still drifted. On my own level were the birds. A black-backed gull flew by, very near, its wings making a flap-flap noise like a book being shut several times in succession. There were other birds I did not recognize, but once I saw a puffin, perched on a stone much higher up, solemn and judge-like. I continued the journey—arms, legs and sweater now filthy from the rock. At last I was on the wide shelf one hundred and fifty feet up, where the diagonal flaw ended.

Here was the surprise of the climb—a cave. It extended back no more than a few feet, and it was not high enough for me to stand upright, not much more than a black hole. I sat down, cross-legged, in the entrance and peered at the walls; they were just slightly redder than the prevailing grey stones, as was the dust on the floor. A man could live here. I remembered childhood games of imagining myself locked in the lavatory for ever and ever, of how I would pass the time by fitting up shelves and storing food, or building a cupboard for toys; there would be room for the bread-bin down on the left side of the pan, for orange squash bottles in that crick of the pipe where the Harpic was kept. So, too, here I could bring up food in my pack and hide for weeks. It wasn't impossible; men had lived in worse places. There was no sign, however, of anyone having tried it here. There were bird remains all over the ledge outside, just like further down. It seemed to be a favorite nesting site, for there were not only feathers, but bits of twig, skeletons of small unidentifiable creatures, and white and yellow shit stains all across the stone.

The sea breaking on the rocks below was out of sight under the overhang, so its sound, too, was cut off. Instead of the restless falling and gathering of white waves there was this grey-blue sheet stretching out below, heaving and wrinkling; I could almost hurl myself down there, I thought, and its embrace would be like soft blue wool. I looked up to avoid the growing insistent pull of the drop, and wondered if it was possible to climb any higher. There was no immediately obvious route. The cliff rose sheer, though there were buttresses and pinnacles of rock to cling to in places. I thought again of the mighty crash that had caused it all. Had one half of the hill really been ripped away?

Frost might have been the cause, or ice cracking the weak points in the rock structure. I imagined the noise, the segments of stone splitting off, the landslide of earth, the terror of prehistoric beasts caught near it. There could even be dinosaur relics fossilized in this stone; some of its crazier shapes were like the faces of nightmare monsters.

The cave, this central point of the cliff to which the path had led, might have been the home of some ape-man, an agile, hairy precursor of myself, who could slip with ease up the crack I had just laboriously climbed. I took off my sweater. It was incongruous here, with this landscape, sea and sky, to wear such a civilized thing. I had bought it in an expensive shop, ages ago. The floor of the shop had a carpet; assistants padded over it in bright black shoes and neat dark suits: "Can I help you, sir?" I pressed my arm against the stone. Despite its rough texture and durability, I would shin up the rest of it regardless of any power it had to hurt. I would almost welcome the fight with it, the rock trying to tear and scratch at me.

I lay on my front and leaned over the edge. The tide had sunk all the beach and was beginning its daily battering of the cliff-foot. Life would have ceased before the sea could scour out passages into this rock big enough to cause another fall. The white water drained back under each succeeding wave and as that, in turn, crashed against the cliff, spray surged up, then fell back on the surface, slap-slap-slap. Again it happened. Again. Again, again, again.

It was a long way down. I imagined myself falling. It would be certain death down there. And I've only just found a lover, a *real* lover! The slow painful growing was finished; the body-machine was developed to its peak, and the mind was stuffed with all the requisite labels and certificates. Life has only just started! This death would mean pain; there would be no gentle slipping into the white lace of the waves, or, as I had imagined earlier, sinking in blue wool. Drowning, suffocation in water: I remembered fish on a river bank, uncontrollable spasms as they asphyxiated in air. Worse would be the rocks, shattering bones out of their patterns of joints, or the smash of light as the face met stone, or being impaled, the pinnacle ripping up through me.

Gary, I love you. Help me!

I pushed back from the edge and stood up. These things were not going to happen; they were only fantasies, and like so many fantasies about death or violence done to me, they ended with worries about remaining alive, maimed or paralyzed for life, weedier forever than the next man. How was I to climb higher? The rocky face stretched up, but the ledge I was standing on was not wide enough for me to be able to see the top of the cliff. A bird hovered in the sky, a buzzard perhaps, and above it, the clouds still moved majestically inland. My sweater. I put it on; it was clammy with cool sweat.

There were three or four obvious holds to begin with; in a matter of minutes I was high above the ledge and the cave disappeared from view. Then trouble started. I was right up under an overhang, and the sensible course was to return to the ledge. Suddenly I was afraid. Going down, now that I thought about it, presented all sorts of difficulties; I would have to keep both hands and one foot firmly in the slits the cliff afforded while the other foot stretched out, stubbing for a fissure lower down. Suppose I did not find it? Or if I found the wrong one, how could I tell whether it was safe or not? I imagined the loose rock crumbling, the feet sliding out into space, and the arms, caught by surprise, unable to sustain this sudden lurch of the body, and I would be hurtling through air. For a moment or two I was frozen with panic, and I crouched up under the overhang, too terrified to look at the sea. I would not go down, I decided, under any circumstances, even if it meant the indignity of waiting for Gary and a search party. Perhaps I could edge myself sideways. There was a handhold to the left, and a tussock of grass. Grass was normally not to be trusted at all, but this time it would have to be; there were no footholds, for the face was smooth, almost polished. I put my left hand round the grass and tugged. It seemed safe, but it would have to share my whole weight with the rim over which I curved my right hand, and it would have to hold while I hauled myself up. If it broke, nothing would stop me from plunging onto the rocks. Gary's face came into my mind. Gary! The grass held; for a second as I trusted myself to it completely I looked down and saw my bare legs dangling in air, and miles below, the sea.

I was safe, but relief was tempered by the realization of my stupidity.

By now I could have been skewered. How idiotic it was to have come on my own! I had no food, and if it was impossible to climb any further I might starve to death. If I had to stay here for any length of time, my clothes were quite unsuitable, and if I was rescued, there would be all the disruption of the lives of other people who had to come out to look for me, the lectures and moralizings, the uncomfortable feeling of inferiority to wise old Gary, the sense of shame and failure in myself. There was one cheering thought, however: the patches of grass meant I could not now be far from the top.

The going was a little easier, and I scrambled up a gully between tall crags. There were deep rifts in these, so that at times what I thought was part of the cliff turned out to be a gigantic slab or stack, only attached to the main rock structure at its base, soaring up, separate. Some of the crevices were wide enough to climb into; one of them might provide an easy route to the top. At the head of the gully the wall was sheer and smooth, so I squeezed sideways into the nearest of these miniature chasms. It was the bleakest, most desolate part of the journey. Behind and in front were walls of rock, black and damp, and right above at the summit, a long thin track of cloudy sky. It was so quiet that my breathing roared. The ascent now required some considerable physical effort. I kept both feet pressed against the wall in front, and my hands and arms on the wall behind. Very slowly I levered myself up. The boy sweeps in Victorian times must have clambered up chimneys in this way. Eventually my head popped out like a sweep's broom, and I could see at once how vast the sky really was and how far off the sea.

I was bleeding. I had cut both wrists in crawling up that dark slot. There were two tears in my shorts, one six inches long up the side; one rip with my hand and they would fall back down the abyss. One more push; I was out of the darkness of the chasm, and panting on the clayey soil. I'd done it! There was grass, and heather in bloom, and little black eggs of rabbits' droppings. I stood up. For the first few steps, I could not get used to the notion that I did not have to worry about where I was going to put my feet. I leaned over for a last look, and said to myself: I beat you, you bastard; I'm one you didn't get.

Gary had a fire lit. For a moment it was all foreign – another human being, my lover, going about his peaceful pursuits; my eyes were still full of ancient rock-faces and vast panoramas.

"Want some fish?" he asked.

The smell brought me back to the world – chips, wet Friday nights, suburbs. I was hungry.

"Please."

"You're filthy."

"It's a rough old climb." I looked at the fish bubbling in the pan. He had even managed to put breadcrumbs on them.

"They won't be ready for a while; I've just put them on. There're some spuds in the bottom of the fire, too."

"I'm going to have a bath."

I took off my clothes and threw them into the tent, then picked up a towel and walked down to the stream. I was tired now, and arms and legs were beginning to ache; I was looking forward to the time after the wash when I would be warm and dry and full of hot food, and a sleepy, contented relaxation would come as I finished a bottle of beer.

We had discovered the deep pool in the stream on the first day. The icy rushing water was always a stab of pain at first, but it would soon ease. I stepped in, and propping my arms round two convenient stones let the stream pour over my shoulders. My body dangled down in the pool and the speed of the water kept me half-afloat. When I had recovered my breath and the cold sensation had lessened so I could relax a little, I began to enjoy it. My body was rising and falling in the water: it was completely free of my mind and no harm could come to it here. I ducked my head under and opened my eyes: grey flying movement. There could be no drowning in this. I came up, gasping, and shook my hair.

"Dinner is served," Gary said.

The clouds were lifting. The whole coast was visible.

"I said dinner was ready," Gary repeated. "We've run out of beer, by the way."

"We'll have to walk to Hartland then."

"It's five miles."

"What's five miles?" I scrambled out and started to dry myself. "I should be worn out, but I could walk twenty."

He laughed. "Come and eat the fish."

As I ate, I thought of his body, of making love with him, of being screwed. I didn't need to prove my maleness; I was just as much a man as he was. Climbing cliffs and worrying about sex roles; it was a load of macho nonsense. His cock inside me, coming. Tonight I'd *really* enjoy it.

The fire was making me sleepy.

"It's a funny thought," he said, a few moments later. "This time last week you were falling asleep. We'd spent all the previous evening at a disco. Different from rock climbing!"

But I heard little of this; I slept, and my dream was forcing me up the cliff face again. This time the grass gave way, and I fell, clutching it in my hand. I woke, gasping.

The last cloud lifted, and the sun came out for the first time that day.

"Come inside the tent," Gary said. "I want you."

Canes

It would be a perfect afternoon on the cricket field if Mr. Surey did not come out. It was always possible that he would do so, for he considered it part of his duties as Senior Housemaster of Windsor House to inspect the boys' games. Windsor House had won the cricket cup for years and he was determined that they should go on winning; it was therefore very important that fifth-formers should be taught not to drop their catches. Good habits induced early on made a tremendous difference to a senior cricket team.

The boys at the tail end of the batting side, with nothing to do for a while, strolled slowly down to the pond. On its surface were water lilies and there were flowers by its edge, full of summer scents. There was also a heap of cut grass, damp and yellowing; it smelled treacly, like hay. It was good to lie in or throw in handfuls. Bees hummed in the heat. The plunk-plunk of the cricket game seemed drowsily distant, a few white-clothed movements wavering in the hot air. The boys rolled on the springy grass-heap and swopped legends about Mr. Surey—

fables based on truth, but which, over the years, had received improbable adornments. The panes of glass in his door were boarded up so the headmaster couldn't see the terror that went on inside. Surey had been in court three times for assault; he had seduced a boy when Kevin Daniels' brother had been at the school. He never bothered to correct exam scripts, but produced a fake list of marks and burned the papers in the school incinerator. Richie Godwin had found charred fragments of geography tests floating onto the playground on one occasion; there had been an unfortunate southwesterly breeze.

The afternoon passed in sharing shudders. It was a slow, rich, warm day. Up on the field wickets fell; one boy left to put on his pads, another joined the group on the heap of grass. Somebody trailed an arm in the pond, cutting a thin crescent of water through the leaves. The lily stems were tough and slippery and went far down. Near the bottom you could touch the slime.

Mr. Britten, who was in charge of the game, umpired; he was damp and prickly with sweat, weighed down at the waist with discarded pullovers. He was a mild and easy man. Mr. Surey, he knew, would not like to see boys sprawling by the pond, but Mr. Britten did not think it really mattered. His mouth was dry, and he looked again at the pavilion clock to see how long he would have to wait for his cup of tea.

Mr. Surey was behind his desk, writing. On his knees was the *Greyhound Times*. He had been reading it when he heard the knock on the door.

"Stand there." He jabbed with his biro at a spot in front of the desk. I moved towards it. "There!" he shouted angrily, and he jabbed again at the place, uncomfortably near to him. He went on with his work.

There was a long silence. Eventually he said, without looking up, and in a more normal voice, "Stand up straight, Crawshaw, legs eighteen inches apart. Hands behind your back."

"Yes sir."

I was so frightened that I did not dare take my eyes off his face. It was a large puffy face; in the middle of it there was a prim little mouth behind which a tongue sucked at false teeth. The eyes were tiny, black and sullen, like a hippo's. His hair was dark and greased down flat. His whole appearance was neat; not a speck of dandruff lay on the shoulders of his immaculate charcoal-grey suit. I had witnessed acts committed by old Surey that, just to think of, made me go watery at the knees. He had once thrashed Paul Hazell; there were marks on Paul's bum for six weeks afterwards. Paul was tough, the under-sixteen football captain. So what was I to expect? My heart pounded in all the arteries and veins of my body, and I thought of a dying sea-bird I had found once when I was on holiday: its heart had thudded in fear so much that I could almost see it under the feathers.

Mr. Surey stopped writing. He took off his spectacles and put them carefully in his glasses-case. "You dropped three catches in the game last Wednesday," he said. "Do you know how I teach people in my House to hold catches?"

"Yes sir." Everybody knew this lesson. Like most other boys, I had been told of it on my first day at the school. My legs were shaking quite uncontrollably now.

"Stop that miserable quivering! And go and select a cane."

At the back of the room, right in the center of the aisle that separated the two rows of desks, was a table. On it were four canes. They were like exhibits in a museum; you almost expected to see printed cards giving their age and origin. It was one of these canes that had savaged Paul Hazell.

I looked at them, aware of Mr. Surey's eyes boring into my back. Two canes were thin and whippy. They would cut into you with a swish, the sting coming as the bending top part curled round you. The other two were thick; they would inflict dull, heavy blows and leave marks like long rods. I chose a thick one.

"Bring it here." He flexed it three or four times to show me that a thick one could be dangerously supple too. I waited for him to say "Bend over." Would it be one for each dropped catch, I wondered, or two? He made no move. It was slow torture and Mr. Surey was enjoying it. He was mad. Mad!

"Put it back where it came from." He thrust the weapon at me. "Now that I know which one you like I'll know next time which one to use. Is that clear?"

"Yes sir."

I wobbled to the back of the room, feeling faint. When I was free and out again in the playground, it took some time for me to convince myself that I was really alive, unharmed, and not just dreaming.

The night before our next game my sleep was plagued by Surey. He was chasing me round the school corridors waving all four canes and shouting, "Come back! Come back! Come back!" I ran up the main stairs, thinking his old age would slow him down. But he sprinted up, three steps at a time. I dashed into the hall, slamming the big glass door in his face and jumped onto the stage. I found I was in a spiral staircase of old crumbling sandstone; the more I ran, twirling up and up, the more it crumbled, and the closer it brought Mr. Surey. But there was a door at the top; if I could get on to the roof I would be safe . . . I pulled; the door was open; there was daylight. On a huge chimney-pot in front of me sat Mr. Surey. I tried to scream. The floor gave way and I fell out into dark space.

As I woke the joy of knowing it was a dream died at once. The curtains were not open, but I knew from the room's light that I would not be spared today. I had prayed for rain. "Lord, I haven't prayed for years, not since the eleven plus. But please, please, if You exist, make it rain tomorrow." I lifted a corner of the curtain. It was hot, windless, summer weather. Everywhere color showed May rejoicing—the cherry tree was a blazing white cloud; young leaves hung in the hedges like green dust; long fingernails of silver magnolia buds were ready to burst apart.

When the bowling was from the pavilion end I was at mid-on. When it was at the other end I was shifted to square leg. It was sultry, like August. Out on the square leg boundary it was safe: the stumps were so far away that they paled into the grass; batsmen were white figures scarcely distinguishable from one another. The ball was a black speck that once or twice curved across the sky, never towards me. At mid-on, however, I was nearer the problems of life. A good thwack might lift the ball at me; I had to concentrate all the time.

Mr. Surey came out. He made no concession to the weather; he wore the same charcoal-grey suit as he wore every day of the year. He did not even unbutton the jacket. His hair was as tidy as when he had arrived that morning. "Over!" cried the umpire, Mr. Millwall, and I came up to mid-on, feeling sick.

My friend, Kit Stephenson, was batting, so there might be a reprieve. He was no games player, and, in any case, he would hardly hit the ball in my direction; he knew the situation. I liked Kit. He had red hair and a snub nose. We often went to tea at each other's house, did the difficult homework together, and talked endlessly about sex. Not just talk, either. We sometimes did it: two teenage boys wanking. Our favorite place to go was under the stage in the assembly hall. Recently, however, Kit had started to have it with Kevin Daniels which made me jealous, so I . . . well . . . I had it with anyone who was willing. But it was never as good as it was with Kit; we'd gotten used to each other, I suppose. And his cock was enormous: the biggest I'd seen.

There was a loud crack as his bat hit the ball; it was going to pass just to my left at head height. It stung the tips of three of my fingers so much that they throbbed long afterwards.

"Let me see your hands," said Mr. Surey. "Palms up." I showed him. He could see they were shaking, but he did not comment on this. "You have two hands and ten fingers like any normal person. The palms are broader than most. There is absolutely no reason why they should not be capable of catching and holding what is, after all, a relatively small ball. Is there?"

"No sir."

"I'm afraid I'm left with no alternative." He sounded weary, as if the whole procedure bored him infinitely. I think he almost yawned. "Go and fetch the cane you prefer."

I did so. Blood seemed to pour through me and I felt weak. I wanted to go to the lavatory. I could hear the shouts of boys in the playground, the plop of tennis balls on wood, the lighter, less resonant sound of a football's bounce.

"Sometimes I make boys take their trousers down." His tone was almost as if he was sharing a secret. "Shall I take your trousers down, Crawshaw?"

"No sir."

He stared at me until his eyes seemed to sink altogether into the puffy face. "Very well," he said, "I'll save that for the next occasion." He picked up the little towel he always kept on his desk. He sweated a lot, and mopped his brow or wiped his mouth three or four times every lesson. "Move down the aisle. About halfway."

I obliged. "Here, sir?"

"That will do. Bend over. Yes, I've now got plenty of elbow room. Touch your toes. I said touch your toes!"

"I can't, sir."

"You don't try. You don't try properly at anything. That's why you're being punished. Move round a bit so that you're facing the back wall. I want you a hundred and eighty degrees away from my desk. That's it! Stop! Don't move."

I waited for the sound of his chair being pushed back, the footsteps down the room, the whoop of the cane through the air. Nothing happened. The silence in the room was absolute. What had gone wrong? I turned. He was still sitting behind his desk.

Seconds passed. A minute, two minutes. This, I guessed, was part of the ritual—breaking down the prisoner's resistance by more torture—but it was not one of the fables I had heard previously.

"You can stand upright now," he said at last in a friendly voice. "I have some books to mark. But stay where you are; I'll cane you when I've finished. If you start to fidget"—his voice became thicker as he savored the idea—"I'll give you six with your trousers down."

I heard Mr. Surey's biro scribbling away. There were long scratching noises as if whole essays were being erased; there were lengthy writing noises—"See me afterwards" or "This work is utterly disgraceful: detention on Tuesday." "Disgraceful" was one of Mr. Surey's favorite words. I knew many boys who could imitate it perfectly, just as they mimicked exactly the tongue licking round the ill-fitting false teeth. Once he sighed profoundly. Once he said "Tch, tch, tch!"

The sounds of boys at play continued; a voice outside shouted "And balls to you too!" I could sense Mr. Surey's head turning, but I concentrated on the noticeboard in front of me. All of the notices were neatly pinned, a drawing pin in each corner. Surey was always very insistent that each notice should be fixed by four drawing pins. If one disappeared, so that a piece of paper flapped in the breeze, woe betide the class that was in his room when he discovered it.

I read all the notices several times. There were games lists, cricket teams to play in the House matches on the 11th, 13th, and 18th of May. The captains' names were in capitals and underlined in red; the wicket-keepers were marked with a green asterisk. My name, needless to say, appeared on none of them. There was a notice about fire regulations, one about lost property; another advertised last year's school play, *Victoria Regina*, by Laurence Housman. Most interesting of all were the school rules. I could not recall having read them before. Some of them were impossible to enforce—"No smoking, not even in private houses;" others were just absurd: "Movement in the first-floor corridor in the north wing must be in one direction only. Boys must ascend by the northeast staircase and descend by the southwest staircase. Orderly movement is essential at all times."

Between me and the notice-board was the table with the canes. I looked at each cane in detail. One of the thin ones was fraying; round the other an inch or two of grey elastoplast was wound. The thickest cane had a bright red mark along it: the blood of a victim, I thought, glad I had avoided this particular implement, but when I looked more closely, I saw that it was part of the texture of the bamboo. Doubtless Mr. Surey polished it occasionally to make it shine like real blood; it was something else he could use to terrify boys with. He's a bastard, I thought, suddenly angry at the wickedness of it all.

"Come here," he said, amiably, wiping his face with his little white towel. I shuffled towards him.

"I really haven't the time to beat you now," he went on. "So we'll forget about it, eh?"

"You mean—you aren't going to cane me—at all?"

"That is precisely what I mean. But if there's a next time—and I'm sure there won't be—I'll do it properly. Trousers off."

"Thank you, sir. Thank you! May I go, please, sir?"

"Yes, of course." He waved me away as if nothing in the world had happened.

I searched for Kit in the playground. "David, what's the matter with you?" he asked. "You're shaking. You look as if you've seen a ghost!"

I told him what had happened.

"Dirty bugger," he said. "Dying for sex with us and he can't have it, of course. So he uses a cane on our backsides instead. It's disgusting!" A vein in his temple throbbed: he was really angry. Then he smiled. "I've got an idea. Look . . . I'll meet you under the stage. I'll be there in five minutes."

It wasn't two boys simply wanking this time. We lay on some old dusty curtains and he held me tight, kissing the terror out of me, stroking my skin until I stopped trembling and was totally relaxed. He took my cock in his mouth. I'd never been so excited, so turned on. He pulled something out of his school-bag. "Shoot into that," he said. It was Surey's towel.

"Kit!"

"I thought we'd give him a little present. It's what he wants and never gets, isn't it?"

"When did you swipe that?"

"Just now. And I've just got time to put it back before the bell rings. I'd love to see the expression on his ugly mug when he realizes what he's got on his face! Shame we don't have him this afternoon."

It was the best orgasm I'd ever had: I thought I'd never stop coming. "Next time you're at my house," Kit said, as he wiped us both with Surey's towel, "and providing my mother's out, I want to take you to bed. Properly."

"Properly?"

"I want . . . to screw you."

"Have you gone off Kevin Daniels?"

"He's useless."

I never heard what happened when Surey next used his towel. I didn't know anyone in the classes he was teaching that afternoon, so I couldn't inquire. It didn't matter; I felt I'd given him what he deserved — and what he really wanted. There was also a bonus: on Wednesday afternoon that week it rained in torrents. A tremendous summer storm.

Cricket was cancelled.

Plums

Mrs. Rainey asked her nephew Clive, his friends and his brothers to pick the plums in her orchard. Since her husband's death she hadn't been able to manage things like that herself.

"Try not to eat them," she said. "I'll give you all as many as you want afterwards. If you start eating now you'll never pick any for me."

"Yes, Mrs. Rainey," they chorused.

The orchard was a wilderness. Grass and thistles were waist-high; each step the boys took was a struggle in an ocean. Dandelion fluff and dust and seeds from the grass made them sneeze. Clive disappeared completely for a moment: he had tripped over a rabbit hole. A blackberry bramble latched onto Graham's right arm: he tugged and a long curve of red flecks swelled on his skin. He looked at the oozing blood and swore, then started to climb a tree. It was hot; it was the summer holidays: there were plums to pick—no one could worry about a little blood on such a day.

There were eight boys and eight trees which were easy to clamber up, and soon each boy was astride a branch, plucking at the fruit. Maurice ate a plum. He was the leader; at fifteen the eldest, the one who made the decisions. Mike, a few months his junior, watched him. Maurice's torso was hidden in the foliage, but his long legs in tight jeans dangled down invitingly, and above the top of a branch was his head—black hair and munching mouth. He spat out the stone; it dropped noiselessly into the grass. If Maurice was eating, Mike thought, there was no reason why *he* shouldn't do the same, whatever Mrs. Rainey said. They were egg plums, large and juicy. Mike bit off the top part of one, and feeling with his teeth where the edge of the skin was he unpeeled it in his mouth. The yellow squashy fruit was much more luscious with its skin off. Liquid dribbled onto his chin; a drop of it splashed on the tree trunk. He pulled at the stone; it came clean away and he threw it into the grass. He squeezed the fruit, playing with it over and under his tongue. Going down inside him it was as cool and distinct as a gulp of ice cream. Then he saw Dominic looking out of his tree, shocked.

He gestured obscenely, and Dominic turned away, blushing. Why did they put up with that kid, Mike asked himself. Because he was good at games; he was the cricket captain of their year, a position of immense prestige. Aside from that, there wasn't much to say for him. He was always very concerned to be in sir's good book at school; his hand was always up for every question, and he usually knew the answer. He would never do anything wrong, and whatever he was told to do he did without a murmur. He was not a boy, though, you wanted to fight with; after Maurice he was the toughest kid in their class.

Dominic, Mike knew, would not eat the plums. He would stagger back to Mrs. Rainey with a bulging satchel. Look, Mrs. Rainey, what a good boy am I, Mrs. Rainey! Dominic's the nicest of them, she would say to her friends later; Dominic brought me all those plums and he didn't eat any! Well I never, they would say; he's a good boy, Dominic: he'll go far. It hurt Mike just thinking about it, so he ate another plum. Then another and another and another. Soon the skin all round his mouth was slippery with sticky golden juice. Dominic was leaning out, grabbing at a difficult branch. One, two, three, four: he wrenched the ripe plums off and dropped them in his satchel. Soon his tree would be picked bare.

Mike eased his way along a branch and jammed himself into the main fork. Here he could reach dozens without any trouble. Most of them went into his bag, but he ate several more. They were not quite so delicious as the first few, and one was definitely a mistake; a wasp had bitten much of its underside, but he had it in his mouth, and his teeth were grinding on nasty hard lumps before he realised. He spat it out. Dominic was watching him again, this time with an expression of amusement on his face. Mike turned his back and climbed away into another part of the tree.

At the far end of the orchard Kit began to sing a hymn, and the voices of Andy and Ian, Clive's young brothers, rose in argument.

"I wish they'd make a plane the speed of light."

"You wouldn't see it if they did."

"It'd still work."

"Wouldn't. Electricity wouldn't go fast enough."

"The current would still be there, stupid, wouldn't it? So it's sure to work."

"How could it if . . . "

Mike was a long way above the ground now. Each time he stretched for a plum the branches swayed and he had to keep a firm hold with his legs. He could see the farmhouse roof and the hay-ricks, black and white cows like toys in the field next to the farm, and, beyond, squares of ripe wheat waiting to be cut, the color of August sunlight. Farther off were the chimneys of houses and factories.

Then came an unpleasant slither inside him. He ignored it and went on picking. Gazing at the soft heavy plum that rested in his hand seemed to make it come again: there was an icy seep of acid down through his stomach. The fruit he held looked a sick thing, and all his innards heaved. It's nothing, he told himself, and stretched out for one more plum. As the trickle spurted into his bowels, he knew that if he didn't race down the tree as fast as the wind, he would have a very unpleasant accident.

In the hedge he found Maurice with his jeans off, his skin glistening with sweat. Maurice's face was pale as a candle and his hair was plastered to his forehead. "Christ, I wish I could die," he whispered, shuddering.

When it was over Mike lay there half-undressed, weak as water. There was a rustle nearby; he thought it was an animal, perhaps the farm cat, and he didn't move. Then Dominic's grinning face appeared over the tops of the tall grasses.

"Hey!" Dominic shouted as he ran back. "Come and look at Mike and Maurice!"

"What are they doing?" Kit asked. "Wanking as usual?"

Mike wished they were: Maurice's big cock when hard was a delight. They pulled up their jeans, and trampled through the weeds and thistles; when they saw the others approaching they were far away from the incriminating spot.

But Dominic had told them, of course. They crowded round, giggling inanely, saying "Pooh!" and holding their noses. Maurice took a swipe at Kit, but he was too feeble: Kit dodged easily. One day, Dominic, Mike thought, I'll get you; I'll remove that grin from your ugly mug, fair means or foul—preferably foul, it'll hurt you more.

Andy and Ian were still arguing.

"Did you know there's a school rule that says the Head Boy can be married?"

"Says the Head Boy can be married? Rubbish!"

"There is! You ask Codrington."

"I will and all."

"He's a fourth-former; he should know. There was one who was married: oh, years back, called Timothy Steer—"

"I bet you a quid it's not true. I bet you five *million* quid it's . . ."

"Let's see what you've got," said Mrs. Rainey, when they arrived at the farmhouse. It was cool in the dark kitchen although the Aga was alight. The cat stretched out in front of it on the flagstones. Mike shivered with the chill, and Mrs. Rainey noticed. "You don't look well," she said. "Been eating the fruit?"

"No, no, I'm fine," he muttered.

She looked sharply at him. "I recognize the symptoms," she said.

"Well, I warned you." She pointed to the kitchen table. "Turn them out on there. You know, Mike, where the toilet is?"

"I don't need it," he insisted.

Dominic emptied his out last. There was already a good-sized heap on the table, but from Dominic's satchel there poured a cascade of fruit; the heap almost doubled, and dozens of plums bumped and rolled down its sides, off the table and onto the floor. He stood back, flushed and triumphant, waiting for the inevitable words of praise.

"That's marvelous!" said Mrs. Rainey. "You've all done very well, but really, Dominic, I don't know how you've managed it! I've never seen so many coming from one bag." She paused and smiled at him. "Now I'll give you some to take home."

"I picked the most," Dominic said to Clive. "Perhaps I'll be given the most."

"You shut your gob," said Mike, "or it'll be the worse for you."

"Now, now!" Mrs. Rainey wagged a finger. "You'll all get the same quantity. Though are you sure you want *any*, Mike?"

"Yes."

"Hmmm. Eyes bigger than your stomach."

He scowled.

They were given exactly equal numbers and it was a pleasure to see Dominic look disappointed. Then Mrs. Rainey fetched cakes and brewed cups of tea; everyone made pigs of themselves except Maurice and Mike, who fidgeted, longing to go home. At last they were let out into the evening sun. Clive and his brothers, who were staying at the farm, waved goodbye from the doorway.

They were a gang of ragged urchins. Skin was smeared grey from the trees; teeshirts were splashed, stained, and torn. Graham had a long scar of dried blood on one arm. There were daubs of dried plum round mouths. Mike's stomach still felt very queasy, and Maurice's face was ashen.

Though the day had left its marks, matters were not yet settled with Dominic. Mike needled him all the way home, pushing and shoving him, making rude comments to provoke him. Eventually Dominic lost control and hit him, just as they were about to cross the stream at

Bryson's Bridge. With Maurice, Graham and Kit helping Mike, Dominic, strong though he was, hadn't a chance. He was dragged down to the water and forced to eat mud. Mike found a plank of wood and dredged up black slime from the stream's bottom; it was oozing and gritty and he pushed it into Dominic's mouth. Then they took away his plums. Some they threw in the river; some they threw down onto the road with such force that the fruit burst open, splattering shreds and liquid in all directions. The rest they jumped on and squashed, or kicked over the gate. There was not one in the end that was fit to eat. They left him, standing in the stream and spitting slime out of his mouth, and yelling the filthiest words imaginable. Then they scattered to their homes, as quickly and as furtively as if they were running from the police.

After that, Mike's attitude toward Dominic changed completely. He felt a sense of guilt — the revenge had been sweet, but maybe it had gone too far; it was what they had done with the plums that bothered him most. Deliberate destruction of food, he thought, was wrong, immoral: the starving millions.

He treated Dominic as a friend now. Dominic, less goody-goody and less smug than he had once been, responded. Before much time had passed it was Dominic's big erect cock, not Maurice's, that Mike was caressing and sucking as greedily as he had sucked Mrs. Rainey's plums.

Open Scholarship

C ome into my study one moment," said the Headmaster, as he swept along the corridor in his billowing black gown.

I expected some sharp questions about why I was not on the games' field, but no; he smiled, an expression which made him look like a faintly demented parrot. "I've just heard from Cambridge, Morgan. The senior tutor telephoned; he was my tutor, you know, in my first year. They've awarded you an open scholarship." He giggled. The Headmaster giggling was a frightening sight:his eyes whirled uncontrollably and his face went mauve; you feared for a burst blood-vessel. The sound was hysterical, dozens of light bulbs cracking. "You are the first English award in the school's history." The cracking continued. "My felicitations. . .er. . .Stephen." He crossed the room and shook hands with me: ritual, like baptism; I was now of the elect. "Run along and tell Mr. Tyler. He's probably down in the changing-rooms." I was dismissed. Stephen!

The games, colors, and girls of my friends no longer mattered; the liberation and lightness was as theirs, sweeter even – larks rising, wings of joy fluttering inside me. I danced along the corridor, my hands shooting up to touch the ceiling. By the auditorium I had to calm down, for my route was through one door of it and out the other, and the school orchestra was rehearsing the Overture to *A Midsummer Night's Dream.* They played it at an earth-bound, clogged tempo, for its speed was beyond the capabilities of most of the performers. The orchestra was all tinny strings and too many clarinets, and it shook with the elephantine thuds of over-enthusiastic kettle drums. I tiptoed through, and as the door swung shut and cut off the music, the dance inside me resumed with a surge of exhilaration.

There were a few late rugby games in the twilight: it was cold, the temperature just above freezing point, and the frost in the air made me cough after the dry warmth of radiators indoors. It was Christmas week and there was only one more day of school. Yes, I would phone Evan with my news. We'd met last Saturday at a gay club. It was only my second visit to such a place, and I'd gone there nervously and with a beating heart, not knowing what to expect. I'd eyed him up, but didn't dare speak to him. He was attractive: dark hair and blue eyes. Eventually he came over to me and spoke, asked me to dance. He was nineteen, a year older than I, and he worked in a bank. We spent the whole evening together, and, when we left the club, had sex in his car. We exchanged phone numbers, promised to meet again. I could, he said, if somehow I was able to invent suitable lies for my parents, stay with him next weekend. I had never made love in a bed before, never slept with anyone all night long. I was as excited at the thought of it as I was about my Cambridge scholarship. And would this develop into an important relationship; would it be long-term or not? There was all this to find out. The first hurdle had been achieved, however – my parents said I could stay in London on Saturday night. I wanted to go to the theatre, I'd told them, and this friend had suggested I sleep on his sofa; the play finished so late.

I ran past the science building and across the forbidden first eleven cricket square, forbidden, that is, to six hundred and twenty-seven boys out of six hundred and thirty-eight, including me; but I could afford now to disregard all holy writ. The damp steam of the changing-room wreathed over me as I opened the door. The first fifteen were mucking about in the big stone bath; the term's last game was over and it was time for foolery. Hot wet flanks and loins loomed through the mist; there were splashes and slaps and legs thrashing. The steam was so dense it was impossible to relate thigh and fist and head correctly, though I could identify voices singing a crude hymn. A creature appeared near me and clambered out, wet hair plastered to its scalp like seaweed. It became a boy, Kevin North. He buried his face in a thick white towel and rubbed vigorously.

"Seen Fred Tyler?" I asked.

He emerged. "Steve! No, he's gone home, I think."

"I've got an open scholarship."

"Good. That's great." He began to dry his chest and back. We had enjoyed our week up at Cambridge, despite having to work through two exam papers a day. We drank every evening, smoked like chimneys, discussed the most pleasurable ways of having sex, cooked baked beans on toast at eleven p.m. and told ourselves we were men. Kevin had been informed two days ago that he had not been awarded a place.

"I'd better be off," I said. "How about some beer tomorrow night? I want to celebrate."

Kevin sighed. "I have nothing to celebrate," he said.

"No, I'm sorry . . . That was tactless of me."

"It's all right." He looked hurt. "I'd set my heart on Cambridge . . . anyway, I'm busy tomorrow night."

"A woman?"

"Uh-huh." He turned away and was lost in the steam. I remembered how four years ago, I had come back here one evening to look for a rugby shirt I had forgotten: hateful days when I couldn't avoid the compulsory twice-weekly physical activity, when being nude in the bath afterwards with so many others was an intolerable affront, a time spent worrying whether mine was as big as the others' or in furtive peeps at their pubic hair, my hands over my own to conceal how little of it there was. The evening I came for my shirt I saw Kevin in a dark corner masturbating with Mike Dewy, and, instead of running away aghast, I joined in and did it with them.

Kevin and I were close friends, but we never alluded to that incident. I looked now at the brass piping of the showers dripping with condensation, and the gleaming tiles of the walls. The crude hymn rose to a deafening climax and dissolved in guffaws of laughter. I went out into the cold, glad that I would never have to go in there again. My scholarship now won, I could leave school this term: tomorrow.

A final whistle blew and the under-fifteens broke up into an untidy dash off the field. The boys of this age were all arms and legs, squashed little bodies between lengthening limbs. Their cries rang through the clear air. My breath spiraled up; already the evening's frost was printing silver dust on leaves and blades of grass. In the distance the Head was hurrying to his car, his black overcoat and black bowler making him a silhouette against the silver grass, an animated cartoon figure. The sound of his engine, chilly and unwilling, carried across the field. I thought of the uncomfortable house where he lived, ten minutes away; he had entertained the sixth-form with coffee and biscuits there once, an embarrassing and silent occasion, thirty of us lolling awkwardly on stiff Victorian chairs and flower-patterned sofas, trying desperately to think of suitable subjects to discuss.

In the street I caught up with Fred Tyler. Most of the work which I had regurgitated in the scholarship exams had been spooned and shoveled into me by him. I should have been grateful, but we didn't get on.

"You examine well," he said, twice. "Remarkably well."

It suggested a limitation on the extent of my achievement. I did not thank him; instead, I told him I would be leaving tomorrow.

"Really?" he said. "To do what?" But he didn't listen to my reply.

Fred Tyler lived in a bachelor flat not far from the school, and I'm fairly sure he was gay. I haven't got much evidence but he certainly took more than an academic interest in a boy in my class called Colin Plumridge. And I think he knew I was gay. Two years ago he'd nearly caught me in the act: I was in that same dark corner of the changing-rooms where I'd found Kevin and Mike Dewy, my fly undone, Colin

Plumridge kneeling on the floor, my cock in his mouth. We heard someone approaching. In the nick of time Colin was on his feet and my cock was safely inside my trousers. Fred Tyler! My hand was still zipping up my fly, and the bulge of my erection was obvious; also we must have looked extremely guilty.

"You know you're not supposed to be in here this late after school," Fred said. "Get out."

Since that time he had treated me with a reserve that was little short of open dislike. But he was still friendly with Colin. Too friendly. He was jealous, I guess.

I watched him speed away down the street. His walk invariably suggested that he had urgent business to cope with; like Chaucer's sergeant of the law he "seemed busier than he was."

On the way home pinpricks like Fred Tyler stopped hurting, and I gave myself up to wallowing in self-satisfaction. Titles of erudite books floated before me—"The Golden Bowl—an Annotated Edition," and "The Nineteenth Century Dilemma: a Critical Study of Dante Gabriel Rossetti," both by Stephen Morgan, whilom scholar of Queens' College, Cambridge.

I went into a telephone booth and, my heart beating a little faster, I dialed Evan's number. I saw his face, in my mind's eye, as it was last Saturday in the car, his kisses, his fingers exploring my skin. Coming. As I waited for him to answer the phone, I said to myself: I am an adult now, free of everyone and everything; I can do exactly as I please. I am free.

The Queen of Queens

Once upon a time, long before I arrived in Exeter, there was a classics don at the university called Hubert, who drank in the gay pub—*The Mare and Foal* it was then—and who invented nicknames for many of the customers. These nicknames were mostly female, and they described, so I'm told, the men they were given to with an accuracy that was quite wicked. It sounds a bit like homosexual life in Granddad's time, when simpering camp rather than aggressive clonery was the image by which we ("queers" then) were thought to identify each other. Hubert disappeared ages ago to a disgruntled and solitary retirement by the sea at Budleigh Salterton, but the nicknames have endured—Doris, Matilda, Lottie, Coral, The Maidenhair Fern, The Lady Davinia, Lydia Languish—like signposts pointing to places that exist no more, or words in an ancient ceremony that have long since lost their meaning. For the pretty young chickens that Hubert christened are now middle-aged and their greying hair is as short, their shirts as plaided, their faded jeans as tight, their moustaches as bristling as any clone on Castro or in the Coleherne. And instead of Campari glasses lifted in delicate fingers, they now swill down their beer in pints firmly gripped in masculine fists.

They don't object to the continuing use of their nicknames, provided they're mentioned only by friends, and jokingly at that; Coral, indeed, would be rather hurt if he was simply referred to by his real name, Graham Smith. Tony Boyles, however, has always objected to being Lydia Languish; so the rest of the world, unkind as it is, has invariably called him Lydia. Of all Hubert's baptisms, Lydia is the only one employed by everybody, friend and foe alike, to his face and behind his back.

It's so indubitably right, for some reason or other impossible to explain. Doris and Matilda and Coral aren't right – now. They're pleasant, ordinary people, neither happier nor unhappier, more interesting or less interesting than most of the human race, fun at parties, sympathetic when you're down; warm, affectionate men. Lydia, however, is different. A real queen. The queen of queens.

His appearance, for example. It changes more dramatically than the French governments of the Fourth Republic. Moustaches come and go every few months; hair color alters with the time of year just as the green leaves of July turn brown in October. A perm is straightened in March, a beard discarded in August. And the clothes! Never the same from one week to the next. His wardrobes must be huge in size and vast in number. When we all had Saturday Night Fever, his white shirt and white trousers were immaculate, his gold medallion glittering on his suntanned hairy chest; when *The Sting* was *the* film we had to rave about and see at least twice, Lydia sported thirties suits, a straw boater, a floppy bow tie, and a stick. And in summer there is his yachting uniform – neat blazer and flannels; in winter his three Brezhnev outfits – all-over furs and Astrakhan hats.

As you may have gathered, he's not exactly poor. He owns a small publishing firm, the Ave Maria Press, which specializes in Bibles. Despite the recession, there seems to be no slackening in people's demand for the Good Book, which is rather puzzling. Why do all these purchasers *want* Bibles? Do they lose them as often as I lose telephone numbers, pins, cigarettes? Whatever the reason, Lydia is obviously on to a winner. (Wish I was. Well, I am in fact, though I don't mean financially, and Lydia caused it: which is really the point of this story.) Lydia's a regular churchgoer—I suppose, in his position, he has to be— but I wouldn't exactly call him religious. Too fond of the pleasures of the flesh, and I don't blame him. His brand of worship is very high Anglo-Catholic, of course; more papal than the Pope. No end of smells and bells and camp processions with banners waving and crosses akimbo in *that* church, and there's hardly any need to mention that everyone, simply *everyone*, who is anyone at St. Nectan's—head choirboy, church-wardens, sidesmen, curates, vicar, even, it's rumored, the cleaner *and* the nice ladies with Maggie Thatcher hairdos who arrange the flowers on Sundays—is as gay as a brush.

Lydia's taste in men is very similar to mine, and I've often envied him his luck. Or cheek, or money. More than once, oh many more times than once, he's swished out of the pub and popped into his brand new Lancia, or TR 7 or whatever the latest chariot may be, the cute blond I'd been chatting up or buying lager for the whole evening. Not always, though. I do have my moments. But Lydia is ten years older than me! Forty-five! He's remarkably well-preserved, of course. He can afford to be. "David, how does she do it?" people ask. "She's wonderful! Considering how old she is."

Successful in the bedroom, but he has almost no friends. Kevin Sullivan is about the only one, and I imagine, being acquainted with them both, that Lydia is seduced by synthetic charm and Kevin by the trappings of affluence. "He's the one guy I know," Lydia said, "whom I could live with." Which made Kevin's ex-lover, Jack Crawley, shout with laughter. "In less than a week," Jack said, "they'd be bashing each other's brains out with Lydia's precious art deco porcelain."

The absence of friends in Lydia's life isn't the result of his posturings, people disliking them, or not being able to stand the competition—but because he is most of all a queen in the way he treats everyone. A more moody, bad-tempered person would be impossible to conceive of. Lovers get thrown out regularly, if the coffee they bring him in bed is lukewarm, if they don't want to watch a particular TV program, or because they've been there too long: a fortnight Lydia feels is an adequate length of stay. Occasionally, *they* leave *him*. "Lydia Boyles is useless in bed" was at one time to be seen, in letters six inches high, among the graffiti in Exeter's most patronized cottage: evidently the parting shot of a dissatisfied customer. Jack was once foolish enough to commiserate with Lydia after a man had walked out on him. Lydia was furious. "Who told you? What business is it of yours? How dare you!" were his reactions.

"I was only trying to be sympathetic," an astonished and bewildered Jack replied.

"Fuck off elsewhere with your sniveling sympathy!" Lydia screamed.

Jack should have known better. But he's a poor judge of people.

Lydia, I have to admit, could be quite amusing about his lovers. "Saturday, I have to go to Birmingham to screw Richard," he said. "Sunday I'll be in Cardiff screwing Peter." He paused, and sighed, a long, long sigh that expressed all the weariness of the world. "What a waste of petrol it is!" It was the only time he managed to make me laugh. Usually, when I hear of yet another break-up, I feel a certain amount of disgust. Rob, the most attractive and interesting of all of Lydia's boys, stayed longer than the others: Lydia nearly fell in love with him. They went on holiday, to Mykonos. Lydia's birthday occurred when they were away, and Rob bought him champagne, an enormous box of chocolates, and strawberries. (Where, on Mykonos, he's found strawberries in September I can't imagine.) On the birthday morning, Rob woke him with a kiss, wished him many happy returns, and gave him the champagne, the chocolates, the strawberries. "Can't you see I'm trying to sleep?" Lydia said. "Fuck off!"

Some months ago, he came to me with an interesting idea. Would I consider joining him in a business venture? Those Bibles were getting on his tits; he wanted to start a new firm that would specialize in gay fiction. It was a hole in the market, he said; there was a need for it, a demand for it. The existing gay publishers did all the serious things very adequately: the political, historical, sociological stuff, and they also did a few quality novels. But in Britain there was no outlet for gay Mills and Boon or same-sex Barbara Cartland. Yes, we were still in the grip of a recession, and publishers were shrinking rather than expanding, but in this particular area one could only expand: a nothing couldn't shrink. He was more than enthusiastic.

I've been in books the whole of my adult life. Owned a book-shop once. Dabbled in all kinds of writing—travel, biography, short stories, reviews, a regular column in a newspaper, lit. crit. contributions to academic magazines. And I've worked for more than one publishing house.

I was, I guess, the obvious person for Lydia to approach. But I was surprised, indeed astonished. He knew what I thought of him and vice versa: we weren't friends. We'd fall out in no time, particularly if we hired as an assistant any attractive young blond. "It would be a purely business arrangement," he said, as if he was reading my thoughts. "We wouldn't have to see more of each other than is absolutely necessary. I'd handle the whole business side of it, of course. You'd be the editor, have the sole right to decide what we actually accept. And you'd be good on publicity. You've got flair, imagination, talent. And you work very hard." He sounded like an omniscient headmaster delivering an end-of-term report.

"I'll think about it," I said.

I did think about it. My initial reaction was to dismiss the idea as ludicrous, but I changed my mind. Lydia undoubtedly knew the art of making money, and he was right, I discovered when I enquired of gay people I knew in the book trade; there *was* a hole in the market. We couldn't go wrong, they all said.

Some weeks later I phoned to tell him that I thought it made sense.

"Come over for a meal, and we'll discuss the details."

Dinner at Lydia's plush Georgian house proved to be a very pleasant experience. I hadn't been there before; I was extremely tired that night, and almost put him off, but I was glad I didn't. The food—he's an excellent cook—was superb, and the drink splendid in quality and unlimited in quantity. His taste in furniture and decor was impeccable. Business, in fact, didn't occupy much of the evening. He wasn't interested in my thoughts about who and what we might publish; "I leave that to you," he said, with a sweeping wave of his hand. What we would call the new house was chiefly on his mind. We went over this at some length, but came to no conclusions. "David, I must have a decision by Monday," he said, eventually, in very managing director's tones. "I want to register the company next week. So think about it tomorrow, and you'd better come up with a *good* idea."

One reason, perhaps, that he didn't want to spend a great deal of time on business was the presence of another guest, Ulrich. I assumed at first that this young blond German was a new lover, though he wasn't being treated as a glorified house-boy, which is what Lydia usually requires of his men, but as a real guest, like me. He was an *ex*-lover.

I phoned the day afterwards with some possible names for the firm, but Lydia was more interested in finding out whether I fancied Ulrich or not.

"No," I said. I'd been too tired to let the young German make any strong impression of that sort, though he'd seemed bright, intelligent and amusing. And at twenty-four, older than he looked.

"Well, he didn't fancy you either." Lydia sounded petulant.

So what, I said to myself. It was likely, however, that I would meet Ulrich again. He had been working in London—which was presumably why I hadn't seen him with Lydia when they were lovers—but his job had recently moved to Exeter; he was staying at Lydia's until he found somewhere to live. He was a bookkeeper, employed by a firm that sold office furniture.

Nothing happened for a couple of weeks; then Lydia rang to say that he hadn't registered our partnership yet: we still had to come to a final decision about the name. He made it sound as if it was my fault. I got the impression that he was going off the whole idea, other irons in the fire perhaps. "Come over to dinner," he said. "We'll have some more talk about it."

"It's really your turn to come to me."

No, no, that wouldn't do at all: driving twelve miles on a snowy December night was far too butch for Lydia. "You live so far away," he complained. About a quarter of an hour by car, in fact; a good, ice-free road for most of the distance. "In any case, Ulrich is still here," he added.

I didn't have any objections to another free meal at Lydia's expense, particularly if it was going to be as gourmet as the last one. It was. But I was right, I felt, about his losing interest in doing business with me. We discussed a possible date for the publication of our first book, but he wasn't as enthusiastic as he had been. And there was no urgency now to have the partnership registered at once.

At eleven o'clock he stood up, yawned, and said, much to my surprise, "I'm tired, and I've got an extremely busy day tomorrow. I'm going to bed." His voice was almost off-hand. "Why don't you stay the night? You can sleep in the spare room with Ulrich. Ever since he met you he's been dying to grab hold of the bulge in your knickers."

Which is what happened, despite the long, embarrassed silence Lydia left behind him. And very good it was. I hadn't guessed before I saw Ulrich naked how much my type he was, physically. Slim smooth boy's body, like a sixteen-year-old: superb firm legs, golden hair all over. But there was nothing adolescent in his sexual performance. That showed a long history of uninhibited adult experience.

It was three a.m. before we slept.

In the morning, when Ulrich was ensconced in the loo, I went downstairs to the kitchen, wrapped in one of Lydia's extravagant bathrobes. He was fussing around, making breakfast. "How was it?" he demanded. I didn't answer, but he knew from the expression on my face. "I could have told you before," he said, "if you'd ever bothered to ask." He pushed a cup of coffee in front of me. "I must fly in a minute, but you needn't hurry away."

I took the hint, so much so that I was still there when he returned that evening. Ulrich and I had gotten up between whiles, for food and to dash across the street for some beer at lunchtime: man cannot live on sperm alone. He was as delightful a companion as he was a partner in bed, mature, but with all the attractive qualities of youth — enthusiasm, optimism, a passion for things, people, ideas. We argued like mad about every subject under the sun. And *he* was chasing *me*! Ridiculous, when I think that I'm ten years older. It was the week before Christmas: that seemed to add yet another dimension to the pleasure.

Lydia, however, was far from thrilled to find me in his house, particularly as I was still in his bathrobe. He didn't exactly say what he thought, but he looked like thunder personified. At any moment he would indulge in one of his famous tantrums: discover something in the kitchen to complain about (an unwashed spoon would be sufficient) and start to fling saucepans all over the place. It was as if he was saying, I let you have one night — just to show you what good taste I have — and you've pinched more than I offered. It was another way he was always losing friends: he liked to put them in certain corners of his life and he expected them not to move until he gave them permission. They were pieces on a chessboard, not allowed an independent existence of their own.

So I beat a hasty retreat.

My only communication with Lydia over Christmas and the New Year was one brief phone call. I rang him, again about the name of the firm. I'd had what I thought was a brainwave, but he snorted with disapproval. He was almost openly rude during the whole conversation. Ulrich, on the other hand, I saw a great deal. Most hours of every day. The simplest answer to the problem of finding somewhere to live, I suggested, was to move in with me. Which he did. Waking on Christmas morning, that gorgeous boy in my arms!

Lydia was not amused. Furious, in fact; word came to me on the grapevine, the local gay-go-round, that unless Ulrich left my house at once he would not only abandon any thought of a business relationship with me, but he would never speak to me again; ignore me in the pub, cut me dead in the street. He was obviously hoping that by the same means — the gay-go-round — he'd get a message back, but whether he expected a fuck-off or an abject apology, yes Lydia, no Lydia, three bags full Lydia, I had no way of knowing. Hold your fire, Ulrich advised, and I did so.

There was now no wish on my part to publish books with him. It didn't matter too much; life didn't depend on it. It was a good idea, and I might explore its possibilities at a later date with somebody else. Meanwhile, I have plenty of work in hand. And Ulrich. Who met Lydia, by accident, one day in January: Lydia was all smiles, all charm.

Ulrich, it seemed, was held to be totally without any responsibility for what had happened. "It's absurd," he said to me that evening. "*I* made the moves; I was determined to try my luck. Who wanted to ask you to dinner that second occasion? Me. And, my God, did he need a lot of persuading to invite you! Yet I'm supposed to be blameless! I don't understand."

"Nor do I, and it isn't worth wasting our time trying to understand," I said. "He's a neurotic. A queen."

In February, Lydia lost patience and wrote to me. It was a remarkable document, John Paul *ex cathedra* in full ceremonial gear, casting out an apostate. *Ite, maledicti, in ignem aeternum.* But it ended with a paragraph suggesting that if I was indeed very sorry for my sins and truly repentant, I would not be shut forever from the source of divine light and goodness; we could, on certain conditions, gingerly pick up the threads. But before he got round to that bit, I was accused of everything evil that he could think of. His typewriter, to judge from the spelling errors it had perpetrated, was an equal partner to his rage. I was aggressive and competitive in my friendships, supportive of no one, untrustworthy, unlovable, unintuitive, dislikeable, egotistical, insensitive: you name it, it was in that letter. I didn't understand him (Ulrich apparently did), and he would never, never consider going into business with me: I would regard it simply as a big ego-trip and when the firm collapsed, as it inevitably would if I had anything to do with it, he would be left to salvage the pieces. So on, and so on. The most extraordinary aspect of the letter, I thought, was that he wanted a reply. I was certainly not going to allow him the luxury of any kind of answer to such hysterical rubbish; what, give him an excuse to snap off my head a second time!

I discussed it with Ulrich, of course. Our reactions were identical, but I admired him for the leniency of his judgments. Not always easy to be fair to an ex-lover.

Lydia disappeared from my life, though I occasionally saw him in the pub. The theatrical way he enjoyed cutting me dead always amused me; the flashing of the eyes and the sharp intake of breath were up to the standard of any bad TV serial, and far from being a method of ignoring me, it spoke volumes.

These drama queens are a dying race. There's little room now for the gay Joan Crawford: the image just doesn't go with short hair, faded denim and plaid shirts. Those who still exist are relics of a bygone era, culture fossils. When they die out altogether, we may even mourn their extinction, for they have a chapter in gay history. But they're certainly a tedious waste of other people's time, a veritable pain in the arse.

What happens to them when they grow old? They embody, I guess, the straight person's stereotype of the elderly homosexual: lonely. Most of us at seventy will either be with our lovers, or, if by default, or luck, or choice, we are not, we will have our friends. Doris, Matilda, Coral, Lottie, The Maidenhair Fern, The Lady Davinia, and all the rest. Not so the Lydias of this world. For them, the likelihood is the fate of the Duchess of Marlborough in Pope's *Moral Essays:*

> From loveless youth to unrespected age,
> No passion gratified except her rage . . .
> . . . Superiors? death! and equals? what a curse!
> But an inferior not dependant? worse!
> Offend her, and she knows not to forgive;
> Oblige her, and she'll hate you while you live.

That duchess may have been a woman, but she was also an obvious queen.

The Year of the Bulls

In memoriam G.B.R.

Every Taurean I know had a bad year in 1981, myself included. Something to do with Uranus retrogressing, the astrologers said. I don't take much notice of that sort of thing, or so I tell myself. 1982, they predicted, would be Much Better: Uranus was no longer bedeviling us poor Bulls and had moved on to plague some other collection of unfortunates, Ariens I suppose. Anyway, the starwatchers said, Taurus people would be much happier in 1982 and for years to come in their love lives, their friendships, their work, their families, etcetera, etcetera. I hardly ever see my parents and brothers, so the nasty old planet—forgetting I had friends and work—had concentrated all his efforts in 1981 on wrecking my love life. Twelve months of one-night stands, the faint beginnings of affairs that withered immediately, and much vigorous use of my right arm. 1982 has been absolutely different, so maybe the forecasting industry got it right. I don't think in my case, however, that the change had much to do with trines and conjuctions and ascending Crabs. It was my father.

That my father should do anything so spectacular as to alter my love life beyond all recognition is peculiar; he was not exactly the kind of man who tried to disturb the universe. However, gentle reader, at the end of this tale you can decide for yourself whether it was he, or the zodiac, or just One of Those Things. Here's what happened:

December 1981 was the worst four weeks of the whole fifty-two. I'd decided, some time previously, that I'd better get on and organize my winter solstice celebrations in as pleasant and hedonistic a way as possible, because there was certainly no one around who was going to do it for me. The program looked reasonable enough. Marc, my Breton friend, accepted my invitation to stay over Christmas, and when he returned home, two friends from Oxford—Harry and Mike—would be coming to visit and see the New Year in. Pip, whose family live in the next street to me, made the fourth member of the party. Good food, plenty of wine, interesting talk for ten days, and with Marc the likelihood of some excellent screwing. I began to look forward to it all.

But I'd forgotten Uranus. He obviously felt very sniffy about the pleasures I'd ordered for myself, and started, bit by bit, to destroy them. He didn't wholly succeed: he hadn't reckoned with Dad, who evidently pulled a few strings on his eldest son's behalf. Which, as I said, is peculiar. Not that he was at all homophobic—in fact, I don't think he ever really minded me being gay—but he wasn't particularly supportive, either. He was one of those men who opt for a quiet life by doing whatever their wives tell them to do. And my mother *is* anti-gay. (She is religious.) I don't know how many times they took their holidays in the West Country—where I've lived for the past twelve years—but not once did they come to see me in my house. My mother, when I asked her why, said cryptically that she wasn't sure of what she might find when she got there. Did she imagine I'd be fucking on the hearth-rug while she watched TV? My father, on the other hand, said on more than one occasion that he would very much like to stay chez moi. "But. . .well, you know. . .it's your mother," he added, rather wearily, as if that was the explanation for all the ills that flesh is heir to. Which, in his case, it probably was.

Uranus' first tactic was to cancel the Roscoff-Plymouth ferry on the twenty-third of December, which finished Marc's trip across the Channel. Fifteen-love to Uranus; annoying. But Lydia Boyles, in his role as Pandarus, unwittingly evened the score by letting me and his ex-lover, the gorgeous Ulrich, sleep in his spare bed. The following night Ulrich and I stayed in *my* bed. Fifteen-thirty. No, let's say, considering how good it was, fifteen-forty. Next morning (a Sunday) I went down to the kitchen at nine o'clock to make coffee, which we drank in bed, prior to repeating the pleasures of the previous night. Three hours later we were both in dire need of a bath.

"You go in first if you want to," I said. "You're the guest."

"No, you have it. It's your bathroom."

"No. Please: after you."

"I don't mind waiting."

Funny, remembering how polite we were to each other in those ecstatic honeymoon days!

"Why don't we share it?" I suggested.

"Now that *is* a good idea!"

I got up, and ran the water. Ulrich stayed where he was, under the quilt. "It's ready!" I shouted, as I stepped in and submerged myself. At that moment the phone rang.

Ulrich padded in. "Shall I answer it?" he asked.

"If you like. Tell whoever it is I'll call them back."

He was ages downstairs. Odd: it was the first time he'd been here, and he didn't, I assumed, know any of my friends. Perhaps it was Lydia Boyles stirring up trouble.

"It was your brother Gwyn," he said, when he returned to the bathroom.

"News of my father? He hasn't been too well just lately."

He got into the bath, sat on my legs and held me tight. He kissed me on the lips, very gently, then licked a trail down my skin till his face was under the water. His mouth closed round my cock: delicate, loving.

I lifted his head up. "What is it? What was that phone call about?"

"David. . .your father. He died an hour ago. A heart attack."

Game and set to Uranus.

My brother Gareth, at the moment my father's heart stopped, was at Mass. Gwyn was with my mother. I was screwing. It seemed pretty typical of the three of us.

If miraculous powers were granted to the dying so that at the point when life ended they were able to see and to know all things; if my father, in that split second, could have seen his sons, could have seen Gareth receiving Holy Communion, Gwyn eating scrambled eggs and exchanging a platitude with Mother, me, naked, sweating, my arms and legs wrapped round Ulrich, moaning with delirious pleasure as my sperm shot in his arse: which of us would he have approved or disapproved of most? I've thought a great deal about that since. And I'm sure he'd think the way I spent that Sunday morning was a lot more profitable than buttering up Mother or kneeling in a cold, damp church.

I'd never been close to him. On the rare occasions I asked myself what I'd feel if he died, I imagined I would be quite indifferent. In fact, I was stunned. For an hour or two incapable of organizing even the simplest details of life, such as making breakfast. Ulrich saw to all that. I babbled, on and off, about him: little unimportant anecdotes that now seemed desperately important. And saying to myself, with monotonous repetition, there is only one day in a man's existence when his father dies.

Eventually I burst into tears. Floods and floods of tears.

I was amazed by the strength of my grief.

Ulrich cradled me like a baby. He was absolutely marvelous, saying and doing exactly the right things at the right moments. Love began that afternoon. "I'm so glad you're here," I said a dozen times. "So glad. . .so glad. . ."

When I calmed down a bit, the phone calls: to Gareth, to Gwyn, to various aunts and uncles and cousins who hadn't spoken to me for years because they couldn't bring themselves to accept you know what. The how and why and wherefore of death. What the doctor had said, when the funeral would be. And the phone call I dreaded, to my mother.

He died on December the twentieth, but the first possible date for the funeral was New Year's Eve. The delay was caused, presumably, by all the public holidays over Christmas; no reason, I suppose, why undertakers shouldn't make merry in the festive season for just as long as anybody else. The dead just have to wait. "They'll put him in the freezer," said a friend I met on Christmas Eve in the gym. "You pay extra for that." Not as tactless as it sounds; it made me laugh, and I guess I needed to laugh. But another game to Uranus: I had to postpone Harry and Mike's visit. (They were due on the twenty-ninth.) *It* was a difficult game for Uranus, however. The funeral was in London; I'd drive up on the thirty-first and later that day I would collect Harry and Mike and bring them back with me. The evil planet couldn't force me to cancel New Year's altogether, just reorganize it. And there would be five of us now, not four. Harry, Mike, Pip, me—and Ulrich.

Quite a day, New Year's Eve. The funeral was very lengthy. A requiem Mass—my mother's idea—the full works: I've never had to endure so much non-stop bobbing up and down, and my father, had he not been dead and inside his own coffin, the centerpiece of it, the *raison d'être*, would have been furious; he was not a Catholic. A life-long believer in nothing in particular. He was, however, the one person to arrive on time: getting Mother ready to face the ordeal made us all late. Then the burial in a remote corner of an untidy cemetery some miles away from the church. A road-sign—"To the crematorium: pedestrians only"— made me smile, but seeing that coffin at the bottom of a wet, clayey hole was horrible. More tears.

Afterwards, the customary ritual with sandwiches and glasses of wine; friends, neighbors, and the surviving relatives. I spent an hour alone with my mother. She was too shocked and dazed to understand fully what had happened to her. Thirty-eight years of marriage, thirty-eight years of living in the same three bedroom house, brand-new when they bought it in 1943 for six hundred pounds. My father's pipe was

still in the ashtray where he had left it. I asked her to come and stay
with me, for as long as she wanted, but she was not so far out of
her wits as to forget her antique prejudices. She refused.

Late in the afternoon I drove back to Exeter with Harry and Mike.
Pip and Ulrich had dinner ready, and afterwards we went to the Hope
and Anchor to see the New Year in. Then on to a party. It was four
o'clock in the morning when we got to bed. Ulrich. Extraordinary,
no matter how old one is, no matter what stress or excess or tiredness,
with the right person it's always possible to make passionate love.

New Year's Day was quiet and gentle. We ate at home and didn't go
out in the evening, nor was there any need for planned distractions:
the house party was proving a great success. I hadn't been at all sure
beforehand that it would be. Harry and Mike didn't know Pip or Ulrich; there could, I feared, be problems, but the composition of this
group of people turned out to be exactly right for a happy and amusing
few days. In theory we were an incongruous collection. Me, thirty-
five, a writer; Harry and Mike also in their thirties, Mike — an em-
ployee of Austin Morris, Harry — a New Zealander, a salesman; Ulrich,
twenty-four, a bookkeeper, and Pip, out of work, at twenty the youn-
gest. Being gay was almost all we had in common. But that's typical
of gay life outside the big cities. In London, if you're gay and absolutely
nuts about Czechoslovak classical music, it's quite possible, I suppose,
to know ten others who are deeply into Janaček, but in a smaller place
our friendships cut right across the social and cultural barriers. Undoubtedly a good thing, in my opinion.

The wit, warmth and good conversation I had hoped for were there
in abundance. Uranus had lost a game to love.

At about ten o'clock that evening I went to the kitchen to open another bottle of wine. When I returned Ulrich looked round, a puzzled
expression on his face, and said, "Didn't somebody else go out with you?"

"No." I counted up: we were five.

"I'm sure someone went with you! Mike, weren't you on the sofa
next to Pip?"

"I've been where I am for the past hour," Mike answered. He was
sitting on the floor, leaning against the bookcase.

"Strange," Ulrich said. "Very strange."

Pip shivered and put on his jacket. There was a very strong cold draft in the room, though the doors and windows were shut and the heat on; I, too, felt cold. I'd lit several candles, and their flames were upright except for one which was persistently flickering and guttering. We all commented on this, then looked for the cause of the draft, but we couldn't find it.

I kept thinking Mike was a long time in the loo. Quarter of an hour, twenty minutes. I wondered if he was feeling ill; he was rather fond of alcohol and had refused to get out of bed that morning until I'd brought him a stiff double vodka and orange. His lunch had been a pint of rough cider. But that's ridiculous, I said to myself; Mike hasn't stirred all evening. Someone had been to the loo, however, someone who'd been sitting next to Pip on the sofa. I'm going crazy, I decided. Too much wine.

"There's another man in here," Harry said.

"Where? What do you mean?" I asked.

"There's a sixth person."

"I've had that feeling for half an hour or more," Pip said. "Maybe your dad is paying us a visit."

The same thought was in my head. Well, he had told me he wanted to come here, but Mother wouldn't let him. Was it possible? Of course not!

"Why not drink to his health?" Mike suggested.

We did so, and waited in silence for a reaction. Nothing. The ghost, or whatever it was, didn't seem offended. Or amused, or grateful, or indeed anything.

"He's come to see what we're doing," Ulrich said. He and I were lying, more or less in each other's arms, on the floor. "Do you think he approves?"

"It's not a malevolent presence," I answered. "No howls and gibberings. Quite nice, really. Warm, despite this bloody draft. No rattling of chains."

"Your old man wasn't a leather queen?" Harry said.

"I can't exactly see him in the Zipper shop."

"He approves," Ulrich said. "He's asked for an hour off, in order to have a look at his eldest son's private life."

"I hope he doesn't want to haunt the bedrooms."

"You're not into incestuous threesomes?"

"Not at the moment."

"I might fancy him. Does he look like you?"

"Does? Did."

"Do you have a photograph?"

"Yes." I fished out an ancient, battered album. The four of them turned the pages over, asked who this was, who that was. More family anecdotes and reminiscences. They all decided my father was much better-looking than me. Laughter; more wine poured. I wondered what the ghost thought. He was still with us, I was sure, though I never had so much as a glimpse of him, just a feeling he was in the room, somewhere. What would he make of this irreverent gay talk? We were now discussing a lighthouse-keeper Harry had been to bed with, then a chicken Mike was after. *Huge* cocks, nipples, syphilis entered the conversation. No negative reaction at all, no change in the warm, friendly atmosphere.

Eventually Pip said, "I'm going upstairs for a pee."

"Aren't you frightened?" Ulrich asked.

"No."

"Ghoulies in the bathroom?"

"I'll give you ghoulies in the bathroom!"

"We'll come and help," Harry suggested.

"Hold it for you," Mike said.

"The one man I want to hold my cock is at this moment in Boston, Massachusetts," Pip answered. "So I think I'll deal with the problem myself."

He opened the door. The spell broke: the draft stopped, the one flickering flame straightened. We looked at each other. Then smiled.

"That's that," Mike said. "Whoever it was has departed. Left no address."

"Or is having it off with Pip," said Ulrich.

When Pip reappeared, he said, "He's gone, hasn't he?"

"Yes," we chorused.

"Some more wine," Mike decided. He held up the empty bottle. "Goes very quickly with five of us. I brought half a dozen with me: three down."

"We'll drink to his health again," said Ulrich. "I'm sorry he's vanished. I rather liked him."

He didn't haunt the bedroom that night, or indeed any night. I was glad: a phantom presence might have put me and Ulrich off our stroke. He never came back at all. Just that one hour on New Year's Day. What was it? Collective delusion caused by alcohol? My complex emotions about the death transmitting themselves through the ether to my friends? Five people just being silly? Or was it really my father, unsettled in another world?

I keep an open mind on the subject. But I'd like to think it was my father, acknowledging, perhaps, that he'd neglected his gay son simply because he *is* gay, that he'd now learned my life was just as acceptable as any other life. Or perhaps he was curious: what do gay people think and feel, how do they behave, what do they talk about in the privacy of their homes? Did he want to see my lover, decide if he was a suitable partner for me?

On all counts he probably went off reassured. Had given me his blessing. Then used whatever influence he had to do battle with Uranus, so that I could score a crushing victory in the final set of that tennis match. Six months later Ulrich and I are still together. Every night of 1982 we've shared the same bed. A heart-beat away.

The astrologers were right, maybe: for this Taurean 1981 was the nadir, 1982 the zenith. But *I* think I owe a lot to Dad.

Pip

He often said, grinning mischievously, "David, my story would be difficult to tell. Nobody would believe it." Now there's a challenge.

Pip, at twenty, was one of the most attractive men – in looks and character – on our gay scene. He could have had anyone he wanted. But he either didn't know how to exploit this talent or wasn't interested in doing so: all the while I was close to him he was in love with an American postgraduate student at the university, William, who led him in a very unsatisfactory dance. It was a non-stop on-off affair; if they spent the night together and everything was marvelous, I could guarantee that next time I saw either of them it would be finished – for good. Until the day afterwards. The trouble was William was hopelessly disorganized; he worked all night and slept all day, and only wanted to see Pip twice a week for a good fuck. Pip found this mode of existence rather annoying, as indeed many of us would. "He only wants you for your body," we all said.

"I know you're right," he would answer. "But I love him."

William, however, isn't the point of this story. What happened to Pip before he met William is more interesting. He was at school in Teignmouth, the same school Andy went to, where Jack Crawley, had he been there then, would have taught them both. Neither Pip nor Andy knew each other was gay, didn't know they were gay themselves. In fact, when Pip at seventeen discovered his real sexual orientation, he thought he was unique, a freak of nature. Such is our education system in the more rural parts of the British Isles. By that time he was engaged to Christine, one of those dull little girls who still flourish everywhere in great profusion, dreaming of rings and weddings and babies and security and an existence just like Mum's. What they imagine their lives will be like at thirty, God only knows. They don't absorb their ideas of fulfillment and happiness from their teachers, I guess. From romantic novels and teen scene magazines, most likely. Such publications are responsible for a great deal of adult unhappiness. But. . . it keeps the divorce courts in business.

When Pip found he preferred men, it was a bit late to unscramble the wedding plans. He should have done so, but that's easy to say. The pressures for going on with it were too enormous, at seventeen, to resist. They were not so much from his family, who were tolerant, understanding people, but from straight society's straightjacket in which we all struggle from birth to the grave. His first experience with gay sex was three days before his wedding, with a guy he met in a "cottage"—a public toilet. Not that Pip was aware that it was a cottage: he'd never heard the word before, and had no notion of what went on in such places. He went in for a pee, and there was this good-looking type flashing his great big plonker. It wasn't, Pip admitted, a particularly exciting or enjoyable experience—he was too scared—but it confirmed what he already guessed. Then he told himself, it will be O.K. once I'm married. It's just a phase I'm going through. It will all come out in the wash.

The wash, however, was a different color than Pip expected. The marriage didn't work, sexually, though Christine soon became pregnant. After a few weeks Pip was back at the cottage, and not just for a pee. There he met blond Simon, the same age as himself, well-known on the local Exeter scene. Simon had been in and out of many different gay Exeter beds, including mine. This time it wasn't a quick jerk-off or a stolen hour when Pip's wife was at her mother's. They saw each other again. And again. And fell in love. Simon was invited to the flat, and introduced to an unsuspecting Christine. Not unsuspecting for long; Pip told her. He couldn't, he said, go on being so totally dishonest and live with himself.

Many solutions were discussed. Christine was driven by a need, at any cost, not to lose Pip, more, probably, from a horror at the likely collapse of security and prestige than because she loved him to distraction, or because she thought he'd mend his ways and turn into a model husband. A pregnant wife, discarded after six months of marriage: when her friends were flashing diamond rings, or talking excitedly of the latest gadgets they'd bought for their kitchens! Separation or divorce were unthinkable. Simon moved in.

At first, to sleep half the week with Pip, who, for the other nights, slept with Christine. Someone, therefore, was always alone. It was intolerable. Soon they were in the same bed; love-making was now a threesome: then, more and more often, just Christine and Simon. As Pip discovered he was wholly gay, so Simon discovered he could be straight.

At this time, these kids were not yet nineteen years old.

It was a situation that couldn't last. Soon after the baby, Sharon, was born, Pip left home. Simon found this outrageous. How could a man abandon his wife and daughter? He elected to stay with Christine, who decided she didn't really want the child. Pip's parents, who still had two children at home, took care of Sharon; they were able, Pip felt, to give her a better upbringing than he or Simon or Christine could. It seemed a wise decision, and as he was unemployed he spent most hours of the day with his daughter, for whom, he was surprised to find, he had as much paternal feeling as anyone in more ordinary circumstances. He was quite open with his parents about what had happened, and they accepted everything, including his homosexuality, without attributing any blame or censure. Christine and Simon conveniently vanished from his life by leaving the West Country and setting up house in London. Pip began to explore the local gay scene; at last he could be himself.

I saw him from time to time and noted his good looks, but I only knew him as one of the crowd. He was tall and slim, with well-cut brown hair, and an honest, pleasant face. He had very wide hips: "child-bearing hips," his friends often teased. And glasses. He was sufficiently attractive for glasses not to spoil his appearance. "Do you think I look better with them or without them?" he asked me once, and I replied, truthfully, that they made no difference at all. Pip had a certain style: clothes, whatever they were, invariably looked smart on his lean, graceful shape, and when he danced at discos he had a natural rhythm and ease that held the eye. He was also a sweet, uncomplicated person, drew friends to himself, and he had a great capacity for enjoyment.

This happy stage of his life—I ought to qualify that by saying moderately happy, because of the problems caused by falling in love with William—came to an end one Christmas Eve. I was drinking in the pub that night. A big crowd in there, all seasonal and noisy. But Pip was alone and he looked very depressed. "What on earth is the matter?" I asked.

"Nothing."

"Tell me."

He did. The whole story, from discovering he was gay up to the present moment. He was only half-way through when the pub shut, so we went to his flat for more alcohol, coffee, and the rest of the bizarre tale. I didn't leave until the wee hours. Did I want to go to bed with him, I asked myself. Good-looking though he was, I wasn't sure he would do anything wonderful for me. I'd want to screw him, and he wouldn't have liked that. All his experiences had been the other way round, and he didn't at all relish the idea of being fucked. I was surprised: I'd thought the opposite. But there are several perfectly satisfactory methods of skinning a cat; I wouldn't say no, I decided. The opportunity did not occur. As with so many people one wants to and doesn't, it was already too late. We were friends. Strange, the taboo on sex with friends, unless you've done it the first time you met. People are afraid it could spoil things. I don't think it does, though I've only proved that once; I'd known the guy for seven years and we'd always found each other mildly attractive. We spent a night together not long ago, and far from breaking up the relationship it brought us much closer.

To return to Pip. What had happened that day was the unannounced arrival of Christine on his parents' doorstep. She wanted to take the baby out, she said, just for the afternoon, to buy her some presents. Pip's mother was a little suspicious, but she couldn't think of any good reason why she should refuse. Christine and Sharon did not return. Pip called the police: they would do everything possible, they said, to trace her, but they had no power to remove the child as Pip didn't officially have custody. Nothing had gone through the courts. They told him they could only enquire if his daughter was being looked after properly, and they would report back.

Which they did, with surprising speed. Christine was still in Exeter, at her mother's, with Sharon who was safe and well.

"What am I going to do?" Pip asked.

"Christmas is the problem," I said. "You won't have a chance of contacting your solicitor till the twenty-eighth, and perhaps not even then. He could be on holiday till after the New Year. But try, 9 a.m. on Tuesday. You must have the baby made a ward of the court. Then the police can bring her back at once and prosecute if necessary."

"But. . .if it all goes to court, I'll lose the kid anyway."

"Why?"

"Christine's only got to tell them I'm gay and I've had it."

"Hmmm. Not necessarily. Your parents are the trump card: the judge is likely to be more interested in deciding which home is best for Sharon than what you do in bed."

"I'm not so sure of that."

"Without your parents you don't stand a chance. A gay man versus a straight woman! The judge, of course, will ignore the boyfriend being bisexual, or the fact they haven't a penny between them. Horror of horrors! A gay father! Only one thing worse in the eyes of the law."

"A lesbian mother?"

"Yes."

"What a fucking, sodding, shitty Christmas present!!"

I put my arms round him and kissed him. Soft, warm lips. Tongues. "What are you doing tomorrow?" I asked.

"Dinner with my parents. Otherwise nothing."

"Come round to my house in the afternoon. I'm off to a party later on—we can both go, if you want to."

He did. Despite his problems, he was without self-pity and, as I said, he knew how to enjoy life.

We spent a lot of time together over the next few weeks, enjoying each other's company, despite the age gap and the intellectual differences. Pubs, discos and parties were great fun with Pip, and so were evenings at home eating a good meal and watching television. William was away till mid-January, and when he returned I didn't see Pip quite so often. But we met, nevertheless, two or three times a week. Everyone else thought we were having a passionate affair behind William's back. It amused us not to disillusion them. "Be very careful with that David," said Steve. "Don't get too involved."

"Why not?" Pip asked.

"He's dreadfully promiscuous! A slut! Sleeps with all the prettiest boys in town."

"Oh, if only it were true!" I said, laughing, when Pip told me.

A preliminary court hearing was held to decide Sharon's fate, and Pip was granted provisional custody. "Gay father makes legal history," I said.

"They don't know I'm gay," he answered.

"Why didn't you have her made a ward of the court?"

"Because *I* want the custody, care and control myself. I'm not letting some cunt-faced judge shred my character."

"Where's Christine now?"

"Back in London with Simon. The police know where they're living."

In February Pip received another shattering blow which put an end to any chance he might have had of making legal history. His mother, who had been unwell for some weeks, was taken to the hospital. Cancer of the stomach was suspected. Then confirmed. She had no idea of the serious nature of her illness, and Pip's father absolutely forbad his children to tell her. Pip, on several occasions, dropped in to see me after an hour at her bedside, visibly shaken by the experience. The deception he had to practice disturbed him as much as the knowledge that she was dying. He would sit for a while, utterly forlorn and sad, saying almost nothing. Then, with that immense ability for pulling himself together, he would say "This won't do. Let's go out and have a drink," or "Disco night tomorrow. Are you wearing your new jeans?"

I admired him.

"What will you do now about Christine?" I asked.

He sighed. "I don't know. My father tells me I'm better off dropping the whole thing. Let her keep the baby. I'm young; I can begin a new life. He said, why not go and flog your arsehole on the Dilly?"

"What do you think?"

"Of flogging my arsehole on the Dilly? He was joking!"

"I meant about beginning a new life."

"It's an attractive idea. . .in some ways. What do *you* think?"

I didn't answer. My opinion was important to him: I never liked finding myself, as I occasionally did, saying something to a younger person that could, possibly, mold their course of action for years to come. "I'll have to think about that," I told him. "But it's certainly worth considering. What your father said, I mean."

"I am considering it."

"I know you are."

"Well. . .what is there for me in Exeter? I want to get a decent job. Go to London, perhaps. Make something of myself."

"I see. William's out of favor today, is he?"

"Don't talk to me about William! I went round there last night, and he had somebody else in his room!"

"A man?"

"Of course."

"What were they doing?"

"Nothing. But they looked so guilty! I said, honey, go right ahead. Don't mind me; I'm just your fuck-piece. *I* don't count!"

"A straight friend, perhaps?"

"If he was, he'll have learned a thing or two!"

The only contact Pip had with Christine and Simon was the occasional abusive letter demanding money and threatening awful revelations if he sued for custody of Sharon. Christine, apparently, was pregnant again—by Simon. Neither of them was working. Pip did not answer any of these communications, but handed them over to his solicitor, who filed them away, presumably for evidence should things end up in court. The letters upset him a great deal, but he still managed to shrug his shoulders and enjoy himself. He was slowly getting used to the possibility that he might never see his daughter again, and that soon his mother would die. She had been discharged from the hospital, and was for the time being at home, leading a relatively normal existence, though she was now very thin. "In a couple of months I'll be as right as rain," she said. Pip wondered if she knew what was wrong, and was pretending she didn't, misguidedly thinking it would spare the rest of the family any suffering.

The on-off relationship with William continued, but Pip sometimes had sex with other men. "Doing that always makes me feel guilty," he said, "though I know he's a bum and treats me rotten."

"Maybe you like it that way," I suggested.

"I do not! I love him."

"It's time you moved on," I said, answering the question he had asked weeks ago.

"I think so too. But where, and what?"

"London?"

"Probably."

Eventually he made the effort. But he was a fledgling, not ready to fly away from the nest. He got a job in London, working in a hotel, but he was back in Exeter after a fortnight. "I couldn't cope with it," he told me.

"Why?"

"Too many old queens waving poppers under my nose and trying to drag me into bed."

His second attempt lasted two months. At the end of the summer, restless, and pining for William, he hitched a ride home; but William settled matters by taking off for America again. Pip returned to London. I bade him my third final farewell, knowing it really was for good this time. There was a lot of affection in my kisses. Could I have had an affair with him? I was glad that we hadn't tried. I'd have influenced him too much, and felt unhappy about the responsibility. But I'm sorry we never once went to bed. We'd have enjoyed that. Both of us.

Another hotel gave him work: two hundred pounds a month, his own room, free board and lodging. For a young man with absolutely no qualifications, at a time when there were nearly three million unemployed, he had fallen on his feet: his good looks and obvious decency got him something where others failed. He stayed there, returning to Exeter for Christmas and the New Year. His mother was still alive, though very ill. He was more confident, more mature. He hadn't found a lover, but that didn't worry him. "I shall," he said. "Sooner or later. I haven't washed William out of my hair yet."

Good luck to him.

But. . .the cost. It's an immoral world that disapproves of gay sex, yet allows seventeen-year-olds to spawn offspring which a year or two later no one really wants.

It's Sharon who bothers me.

Robin

He had reached the age of forty and never had a lover. For some people that might seem a victory against overwhelming odds, but Robin didn't look at it like that; he had always wanted a lover. He could think of many reasons why he hadn't found one: not coming out till his late twenties; few potential partners in provincial, closeted Exeter; an unconquerable incapacity to initiate anything. "I want a man to sweep me off my feet and carry me into the sunset," he would say. But at forty, unless you're prepared to indulge in a bit of positive action, you're likely to remain distinctly unswept and uncarried anywhere, let alone into the sunset.

Robin's friends didn't find his arguments convincing. He'd had plenty of chances, they would say, remembering this or that occasion when he'd walked out of the pub or the disco with someone very tolerable. The first night would even prove exciting; Robin would arrange to see the someone very tolerable a second time, a third, sometimes a fourth or a fifth. "Just my sort of man," he would say. "*He* made all the advances," or "we drank wine and listened to Mozart's Twenty-first Piano Concerto before we did it again — *very* civilized," or "he brought me breakfast in bed." He needed his men to go through these little hoops, just to make sure they placed a high value on him. Or was it because he was lazy and selfish? Whatever the explanation, no one ever lasted more than a week. There was always something wrong: "*I* had to fuck *him*"; "I'm just a diversion"; "he's married with two kids." Fair enough, perhaps, but often the reasons were quite trivial — "he snores"; "he lets the car door slam."

Why did everybody else, he complained, have a lover? Why was he the only one left out? We didn't, in fact, all have lovers. Many of us chose not to. "David, I don't care if he screws all the dishiest men in town," Robin said. "So long as he comes back to me at the end of the day. Cares for me, looks after me. Is it too much to ask?" Well . . . put like that, perhaps it was too much. Not that we said so to him, of course. We did a great deal for Robin: his soulful, hangdog eyes could make us feel guilty. He knew that. "My eyes are my biggest asset," he often said. So, "come round," we would say. "Don't feel you have to be on your own." As a result, he was invited to more parties than almost anyone else. We liked his sharp — sometimes uncomfortable — sense of humor. We even arranged his men for him. In the gay pub, the Hope and Anchor, he rolled his brown eyes one evening at a stranger he said was absolutely his type — a butch, muscular, moustachioed man who looked rough but who, he thought, might prove very gentle in bed. "I want him," he said. "But I won't get him." It took five of us half an hour to bring the two together and pack them off home. "Well . . .?" we asked, next day. "It didn't work," Robin informed us. "Last time I ever do anything for him!" Phil said. "Same goes for me," said Martin. "And me," said Graham, and Brian, and Andy. But, a week later, we were once again making sure that Robin wasn't left out.

Perhaps we needed someone like that. A yardstick against which we could measure our own worth, or luck, or skill, or whatever, and feel good because we weren't the least successful.

Superficially, Robin's problems were an acute fastidiousness — a relic of his upbringing—and thinking that his homosexuality was a serious handicap. "Of course it's easier being straight," he said. Or "Why should I join the Campaign for Homosexual Equality? They'll never be equal. Waste of time! Anyway, I'm just as equal as anyone else." Which really meant he was scared of joining: what commitment would they want from him? Underneath the fastidiousness was a strongly rooted self-dislike, often expressed as a feeling that nature had played a nasty trick on him. "I don't see why people object to John Inman," he would say. "We ought to be capable of laughing at ourselves." And "Gay people are much bitchier than straights," or more promiscuous, or more heart-less, or more superficial, etcetera, etcetera. Telling himself that being gay was a more difficult job than any other made him feel his unhappi-ness was not *his* fault.

He longed for a lover because the world is mostly couple-orientated; the gay world less so in the big cities, but not in the provinces. It's an easier life, out in the sticks, if you have a lover: the chances of a different hunky man every night are remote. Robin was often jealous of couples, and showed it. He had two lodgers, Alex and Mark, rustic boys from Dartmoor, who'd known each other (would you believe it?) since they were three, who'd first had it off behind the bicycle sheds at the age of twelve, and were still together at twenty-six, several break-ups and reconciliations later (quarrels largely caused by Mark's fascina-tion for any hairy chest or huge cock.) Robin disliked seeing Alex and Mark kiss, or holding hands on the sofa; in fact he told them not to, much to their annoyance. But they didn't leave: they, too, felt sorry for him. And—like the rest of us—superior, and guilty because they were uneasy about that sense of superiority.

Robin, deep down, didn't want a lover at all. If he did, the trivial nuisances—snoring and so on—wouldn't have mattered. A lover would upset the routines of his existence, rumple the immaculate appearance of his tidy house, make demands, be altogether too uncomfortably disturbing a factor. And it would be a tremendous leap into a dark unknown; he simply wasn't prepared to take the risk. There were many compensations—the sympathetic attention of friends, the presence of the lodgers which allowed him to escape the terrors of solitude, the amusement caused by his acid wit. Alex and Mark ran his house for him – doing his shopping, cooking his meals – and organized his social life, taking him out in their car to the pub, the disco, the theatre, the beach. "*We're* going to the ballet," Robin would say, or "*we* went to Torquay," and even, at one time, "*We're* thinking of moving," as if he was referring to his life-long other half. He had everything arranged for himself. Except love.

But would a lover have wanted him for very long anyway? He was a selfish man. A dinner party was invariably cooked by Alex: all Robin had to do was to pour the wine, and the last inch in every bottle went into his own glass. If a friend bought him a theatre ticket for two pounds fifty, he'd pay two pounds forty – "All I've got: ten p doesn't matter." And just as ungenerous in his emotions. Good at visiting the sick – upbringing had taught him that – but hopeless at comforting a friend whose lover had run off with another man. He'd listen politely, but sympathy was always withheld. The friend had only lost a lover; it was less of a problem than the fact that he'd never had one at all. Self-pity had doused the warmth he might naturally have had. Perhaps in London or Amsterdam or San Francisco, a greater exposure to gay life than is possible in Exeter would not have caused him to shrink so much. For there was still a flicker of fellowship; the fire had not been completely put out. Alcohol could make him sentimental, even tearful. "I don't know what I'd do without you all!"

Soon after his fortieth birthday Robin fell in love, probably for the first time ever. The experience was wretched and almost broke him. For the other man – Dominic, a university student nearly half his age – in no way reciprocated his feelings. It's perhaps unusual at forty to fall in love so hopelessly. Life has sufficiently battered people about by that age for them to become inured to the attractions of someone who is likely to offer nothing. It's the province of seventeen-year-olds. One develops, long before one's fortieth birthday, some kind of mechanism that stops the worshipping of the ground on which a straight man walks, that prevents the likelihood of becoming emotionally involved with another gay man – however delicious the blond, blue-eyed beauty may be – until he's been tested in bed many times, until one knows him well, has read his character, seen him at breakfast-time and sitting on the loo, and discovered whether the incompatible aspects are important or not. Even then one can still make catastrophic mistakes. Sometimes love only begins when the affair is falling apart; we realize then that we *need* him desperately, that he's become our survival kit.

Not so Robin. One day, just like that, bang, a bolt from the heavens. Dominic was pleasant enough, sociable, interesting. No blond, blue-eyed beauty, however. They met over a pint of Flowers in a half-empty Hope and Anchor, one damp cold day in April. Robin couldn't avoid doing all the adolescent things. Invitations, phone calls, meetings (accidentally on purpose), walking past his beloved's window at night, longing for the unlikely event of Dominic looking out at the stars. Dominic had a vague idea of Robin's feelings, but could not know how deeply he was smitten – Robin took good care to hide that as much as possible. A total revelation would have frightened Dominic away. Keeping his emotions in check when they were together allowed friendship to develop; it was better than nothing. Or was it? It hurt too much. The invitations, the phone calls, the meetings stopped. Robin stayed indoors more and more frequently, refused the blandishments of friends, avoided the pub. Alex and Mark looked at him quizzically, wishing they could help, but simply by existing – a couple – they made matters worse. Robin withdrew even further; he spent an increasing amount of time alone in his bedroom, at week-ends staying up there all day. He spoke to his lodgers in grunts or monosyllables.

"I can't stand it much longer," Alex said.

"Nor can I," said Mark. "We'll have to find somewhere else to live. This house is like a morgue!"

"We can't leave him! He'll chuck himself in the river."

"People don't do that sort of thing."

"Hmmm."

"But what's the answer? Alex, he's driving me crazy!"

"I think he'll probably go crazy before you do."

"What do you mean?" Mark asked.

"Well. . .it can't go on like this! He'll make himself ill. Have a brain-storm."

"Or get over it?"

Alex nodded. "Or get over it."

Dominic, of course, had a sex-life. He went to the club in Bristol with Andy and Phil and Ulrich and me on a Saturday night to find a boy till Sunday morning: he didn't seem to want to get involved with anyone—maybe he was afraid it might interfere with his studies, or perhaps he was too young to want to do anything other than sleep around. Occasionally, he spent the night with someone he met in the Hope. If word got to Robin, his anger and distress knew no bounds. The anger was never directed at Dominic, but always at the other man. "I shall strike him off my Christmas card list," he said, if the guy was a friend of his.

"Pathetic," Mark said to Alex.

"Absolutely pathetic!"

"You said he'd get over it."

"So did you."

"And now?"

Alex shrugged his shoulders. "I don't know."

"The intensity of it!"

"The rewards of selfishness."

"What do you mean?"

"If he wasn't so selfish, was more. . .outgoing. . .then perhaps it would be different. He'd have met someone who responded. At his age, not to have a man!"

Mark sighed. "Easy for us to say that."

"What are you talking about? You've screwed round this city. Could easily have gone off with a dozen others."

"But I didn't! I always came home to you, didn't I!"

"All you think about is cock."

"O.K., O.K., don't let's start again on that! Please!"

It had to happen sooner or later: Dominic met somebody who was more than a one-night stand. Robin knew this, but he persuaded him-self that there was nothing in it. Dominic and Bob were just friends. The gay grapevine, so good at spreading gossip, was on this occasion careful not to do so. People were genuinely worried about what would happen to Robin if he learned the truth, so they let him believe that Dominic and Bob simply enjoyed going to concerts together. Impossi-ble, however, to hide something like that for long; particularly after Dominic moved in with Bob. But Robin had only himself to blame for the way he found out.

Jack Crawley was leaving England: emigrating to San Francisco. The week before he went he gave a farewell party. All gay Exeter, more or less, was invited: it promised to be a really good evening. His house — on the estuary—wasn't far from the city, but impossible to get to by public transport. Who was going with whom in whose car was a mat-ter of complex organization. Martin and Graham needed a lift: they had a car, but Graham didn't drive, and Martin had been banned for a year. Nobody, it seemed, could take them; all seats were full. "Robin," Jack suggested. "He'll be coming with Alex, but he could drive your Renault instead. He has a license." Jack, remembering that Martin and Graham were not Exeter's most popular couple, phoned Robin to see if he was agreeable. If Martin got in touch directly, he might be given an outright refusal. Though why I'm doing it, Jack said to himself, I don't know. It was only an hour before his guests were due to arrive, and he felt he'd be better occupied with last-minute preparations than solving Martin's difficulties.

"Oh, hell!" said Robin. "If I do that it means I won't be able to drink."

"If you've had too much," Jack answered, "you can sleep in the spare bedroom."

"Bugger Martin and Graham! Why can't they get a taxi?"

"No idea."

"Listen. . .I'm not prepared to do it."

"All right. It's up to you. Not my problem."

"Are you ringing Martin back?"

"Yes."

"Then he'll call me?"

"I suppose so."

"Say we're out. Say you couldn't get a reply. I'll tell Alex and Mark not to answer the phone."

Jack duly informed Martin that Robin was out. He felt extremely annoyed that he'd been pushed into telling lies on behalf of someone who was behaving so selfishly. "What am I going to do?" Martin asked.

"I can't possibly come and fetch you. I'm still cooking. Have you tried Andy?"

"His car's full."

"What about Roger? David? Or Steve?"

"Theirs are full too."

"I don't know what to suggest."

"In that case," said Martin, "I imagine we won't be able to come."

And they didn't. Jack was furious: it was all so petty and unpleasant. Martin and Graham, whatever their faults, were the most hospitable and generous of people. Robin had been wined and dined in their house, and he hardly ever asked them back.

He drank more than anybody else that evening. He passed through the euphoric stage — kisses and hugs and "I don't know what I'd do without you all" — then with unusual speed he fell into a condition of semi-coherent melancholy.

Jack, dancing with him at two in the morning, said "A great pity Martin and Graham aren't here. I owe them at least two invitations, and now I can never repay them."

"Oh. . .it's a lot nicer without those two bitching all night. Where's Dominic? And Bob? Weren't they supposed to be coming?"

"I asked them, yes."

"Why haven't they arrived?"

Jack couldn't resist putting the boot in. "They didn't want to upset you."

"Why should they upset me? I'm not going to throw a tantrum just because they're in the same room."

"They're lovers now."

"What?"

"Dominic is living with Bob."

Robin stopped dancing. He threw his arms round Jack's neck and burst into tears. Not for a brief moment: the tears went on and on. Jack's clothes were dripping wet.

That more or less finished the proceedings. Some people had already gone; it was late: the others were thinking about going, and this moment of general embarrassment seemed a good cue to make a departure.

When Jack called on Robin next day, he was vigorously polytexing his bathroom ceiling. It didn't really need a face-lift — it had been done less than a year before — but painting a ceiling can be very therapeutic. Robin apologized for his behavior at the party. "Unforgivable," he said. "Definitely not British." And he managed a wry laugh.

"Of course it's forgivable," Jack answered. "Much better than bottling it all up."

"I'm sorry about Martin and Graham too."

"It doesn't matter. Are you in mid-hangover?"

"A slight headache."

"Could be the paint fumes."

"I'm O.K. I'll survive." He picked up his brush and resumed his penance.

He never mentioned Dominic and Bob again. They were forbidden words, Alex and Mark discovered. His feelings lessened with time, but he deliberately avoided the places where he was likely to bump into Dominic. He went out rarely, preferring to spend his evenings at home with a glass of gin in front of the television, instead of a pint of beer in the "Hope". He was more gentle as the years passed, content to be a gay old maid, sharing at a distance in other people's joys.

"I shan't find a lover now," he said to me. "I don't even want one. I can't imagine why anybody ever does."

In the Same Boat

Martin was well-off and loved gadgets. His latest craze was a luxurious powerboat which he kept at the marina in Torquay—the mooring costs were a cool six hundred pounds a year, but that sort of expense was no problem to Martin, whose money was mostly derived from his work: he was a partner in a very successful firm of real estate agents. He had bought and sold houses for nearly all of gay Exeter. "The only major crisis on that boat," said Lydia Boyles sniffily, "will occur when it runs out of vodka." Certainly the drinks cabinet below deck was as well stocked as the one in Martin's dining room, but Lydia was speaking out of envy: he had not been asked to spend a weekend on the boat, and all summer long Martin was busy inviting one group or another of us for what he called a "trip-ette" round Torbay and a voyage out on the open sea. He would provide the food and drinks and we could sleep on the deck Saturday night; all we had to bring was our good selves and some bedding. He was a generous man, and I have never heard him utter an unkind remark about anybody—a rare thing in Exeter's tightly-knit gay community, where everyone knows what everyone else is up to, particularly who they're screwing, which is often public knowledge before the people concerned have actually done it. But there was another side to Martin, an exhausting, neurotic energy and an overwhelming desire for status, a niche in society that would impress others; hence the love of gadgets and the delight in showing them off to the rest of the world.

The weekend Ulrich and I slept on the boat there were seven of us—Martin and his other half, Graham; Nick and his lover, Tom; and Douglas, a middle-aged professor from the university who spent most of the weekend marking examination papers. Douglas at forty-five could still have been a fit, trim man but he had let himself go, and, even if he had not, I wouldn't have called him attractive. Attractive certainly describes Nick and Tom, who, though they had been lovers for two years, and had lived in Exeter for longer than that, were strangers to the "scene." Tom was a drama student in his final term, a fair-haired, kittenish twenty-one-year-old with a lovely come-to-bed smile; Nick, ten years his senior and a lecturer in drama at the university, was strikingly handsome—dark-haired with coal-black eyes, and his quiet, introspective manner gave him the added appeal of maturity and poise. He didn't, perhaps, know how sexy he was.

"I'd like Nick," Ulrich said. "What's more, I'm going to have him." I laughed. "You don't stand a chance! Anyway. . .I'd get very jealous." He grinned. "I can deal with that. Why don't you have Tom?"

"I definitely wouldn't mind. But rumor has it that those two are deeply into each other; romantic young love etcetera. No wife-swopping."

The weekend proved how wrong I was: not that events turned out as Ulrich wished for, but it began exactly as I'd imagined. We were late arriving at Torquay because we'd agreed to transport Graham and most of the food from Exeter down to the boat, and Graham wasn't ready. (He and Martin had an odd relationship: they never screwed these days, but seemed to share a house and a bed more for convenience than love or affection.) We found an immense flap going on aboard the boat: cupboards were being searched, the fridge opened and shut, cushions felt under, lockers scrutinized — obviously some extremely important object had been mislaid.

Martin looked up from the bag he was rifling through, and said "You're late, darlings! We've been here an *hour* and drunk all the vodka! But I'm *sure* I put another four bottles somewhere!"

"Lydia was right," I said to Ulrich, and turned away so Martin shouldn't see my laughter. People were always turning away from Martin so he shouldn't see their laughter.

"You left them on the kitchen table," Graham said. "Don't worry — I've brought them with me."

"Oh. . .wunderbar!" Martin exclaimed. "Stunner-ama!"

The vodka was opened immediately, and we spent a very pleasant hour in the early evening light drinking screwdrivers and watching the behavior of the inhabitants of the other boats nearby. The sea was calm, the sunset perfect, and Torquay with its hills, its palm trees, and tanned, happy holiday-makers looked not its usual slightly seedy self, but as glamorous as Key West or San Tropez. Douglas stopped marking papers and drank with enthusiasm, looking young Tom up and down appreciatively out of the corner of his eye. Tom was aware of this but he did not react: he was listening to Nick telling us of the advantages of a strict vegetarian diet — no fish, flesh or fowl and no dairy products. *Spaghetti bolognaise*, however, did not sound to me particularly appetising when the *bolognaise* was made of lentils.

The next crisis occurred when we ran out of orange juice and discovered that there was no tonic or bitter lemon to mix with the vodka. But Martin circumvented the problem by saying it was time to put the boat through its paces. He loved shouting orders — "Stand by, crew!" or "More throttle!" Not my scenario, I decided, so I let the others get on with it and made myself useful by washing up the vodka glasses and stowing them away.

"We'll tootle across to Brixham," Martin said as he steered the boat out of the marina, past the coastguard ship *H.M.S. Active* — which led to a number of suggestions about what might have happened to *H.M.S. Passive*: "Closed for major repairs." said Ulrich. (A private joke — in bed, on occasions I wanted to fuck him and he wasn't in the mood, he would say things like "Shut for remodeling," "Violators will be towed away," "No entry during daylight hours," "Trespassers will be prosecuted," and so on.)

Brixham is a fishing port on the southern edge of Torbay, about six or seven miles from Torquay harbor as the crow flies. I imagined that getting there would be a pleasant little cruise, half an hour on the flat green sea, but I'd failed to take into account the nature of Martin's personality. Once outside the harbor wall, he opened the engines to full throttle, and we shot forward like a rocket. It was the most uncomfortable method of locomotion I have ever experienced in my life: bang, slap, bang, slap as we lifted out of the water and crashed back on the surface; our stomachs rose and lurched; our hands and feet gripped railings or each other to stop ourselves from falling overboard, while Martin, half-sitting, half-standing, twirled the steering wheel as if he were a cowboy mastering a bucking bronco, a smile of beatific happiness on his face. Then, "Look at *that!*" he shouted in dismay. *That* was a powerboat somewhere to our left traveling faster than we were. "Mine's the *fastest!*" he had boasted, a dozen times. I'd have laughed at this moment if my stomach would have permitted, but it did not.

When we reached Brixham I found myself on the deck with Tom in a desperate embrace, arms and legs entwined, though lust, I think, was never a consideration; while Douglas, Ulrich, Nick and Graham were similarly glued together in an unlikely foursome. Douglas unwound himself and quietly started on his next exam script.

"Maybe we can land," Ulrich said. "Have a drink to steady our nerves."

"Why not eat dinner here?" Tom suggested. "There are some good restaurants in Brixham."

It seemed a good proposition to everyone, except Martin. Having achieved what he wanted—"tootling" across the bay—he had to set in motion the next energetic idea that came into his head. Dinner was too tame. He couldn't be still for a minute, and it was the knowledge of that—Martin's presence tiring me out—that had made me pause when he'd invited us. "Oh, come on!" Ulrich had said. "It could be fun." Well, yes, perhaps it could, I told myself; a change at any rate. Feeling seasick hadn't entered my calculations.

So we shot back to Torquay in a matter of minutes; it's just as well I thought, as I bounced around the boat clutching Tom once again for protection, that I put the vodka glasses in safe places.

Martin was finally convinced that dinner was essential, not soon, but right *now*; so, after we had moored the boat, we walked into town and ate at a quite pleasant Italian restaurant. Later, we went on to The Double Two, Torquay's gay club, to dance and drink. The party that returned to the marina at one a.m. still consisted of seven people, but they weren't the same seven. Graham had picked up a good-looking man and decided to sleep on terra firma. "I've spent too many uncomfortable nights on that boat," he said, "and this guy is *cute*. I'll be back for breakfast." Whereas Martin had found a nice young chicken who thought the idea of sleeping on water was terrific.

Martin and friend retired below, and Douglas began to read more exam papers with the aid of a torch. Ulrich and I undressed on the deck and got into our sleeping bag; beside us Tom and Nick did the same. For the brief moment that all four of us could see each other naked in the moonlight, my eyes were on Tom: an absolutely delicious young body. We talked for a long while; the subject was how our respective love affairs started, when and where we had met.

"He taught me in my first year," Tom said. "I fancied him like mad! And I didn't even know if he was gay. . .though I had some inkling."

"It was obvious *you* were," said Nick.

"So why didn't you do something about it?"

"I had qualms about breaking the teacher-pupil barrier."

"What happened in the end?" I asked.

"We went down to Cornwall for the hobby-horse ceremony," Tom said. "The whole department. . .all the students and the lecturers. We hired a bus. There was a spare seat beside Nick, and these girls were giggling about who would dare to sit next to him. So I said 'I will!' And I did."

They were lying together in their sleeping bag, stroking each other, kissing. The boat rocked gently on the incoming tide. I looked up at the stars: it was a night for sentimental stories. And making love. Ulrich's hand on my skin felt good.

"We met under the hobby-horse," Nick said.

The hobby-horse ceremony is held on May Day in Padstow, a quaint little fishing village on the north coast of Cornwall, and is of very ancient, possibly pagan, origin. A man, fantastically dressed in enormous skirts held up by a hoop, dances through the streets all day long and the spectators try to dip and duck underneath them. It isn't easy to do, but success, it is said, means that within a year the virgin will find her true love, the young married woman will become pregnant, the gay man. . .nothing is recorded of what will happen to the gay man. Tourists come from far and wide to see, or take part; the town is packed to the bursting point, and the atmosphere is extraordinary: intensely sexual, primitive—and a bit frightening.

There was a long silence. "Well," I said, impatiently. "What then?"

"After dark I went for a long walk, alone, on the beach," Nick answered. "It was a beautiful, warm night. A full moon."

"I followed him," Tom said.

"We slept together underneath the cliff—"

"When we weren't screwing."

"— and in the morning the tide had gone out, miles out; I ran stark naked down to the sea and found a stick. I wrote I LOVE YOU in huge letters on the sand." Nick smiled, remembering.

Douglas, at the other end of the boat, put out his torch and lay down on the deck. "That's the most romantic encounter I've ever heard of," Ulrich said.

"Pity the rest of it isn't so marvelous," Nick replied, but he did not elaborate on what he meant: he and Tom began to make love.

Ulrich and I did too. "I'd give anything to have a foursome," Ulrich whispered.

"You can't," I told him. "Shut your eyes and imagine I'm Nick. I'll pretend you're Tom." Which turned out to be a reasonably satisfactory way of doing it, and an interesting exercise in self-restraint—Douglas, near enough to see and hear, might well have felt hurt and left out;

so we hardly moved, and as we came we put our hands over each other's mouths.

I woke at half past five, long before the others; the dawn, the open sky, the movement of the boat, had disturbed me. The sunrise was a pink flush over Torquay: silence, stillness. Not a breath of wind. *H.M.S. Active* was now looking very passive, just sitting on the water, comatose. It would be a muggier, more humid day than yesterday; there might even be a summer storm.

Ulrich was fast asleep, his face dreamless, innocent, vulnerable. I realised then, with some surprise, that I wasn't the first to wake up: Douglas' sleeping bag was empty. I turned to Tom and Nick, and surprise became astonishment—Nick wasn't there. A man lay in his place, his arms wrapped round Tom: Douglas. I wriggled out of the bedding, and moved as quietly as I could in order not to rouse anyone; peered into the cabin—no Nick. Just Martin and his chicken, dead to the world.

I picked up one of Martin's many pairs of binoculars and searched the harbor wall, the entrance to the marina, the grass and the palm trees beside the shore road. I saw Nick eventually, sitting cross-legged on the beach, hands pressed against his head. I replaced the binoculars, put on my tee shirt and shorts, and climbed onto the marina cat-walk.

"Are they still fucking?" he asked.

"No."

He began to throw pebbles at the sea, aimlessly. "I wrote I LOVE YOU with a stick. Love letters in the sand: the tide wipes them out."

"Nick," I said, gently, "you don't have to say anything. I'm not being inquisitive."

"I also told you it was a pity the rest of it wasn't so marvelous."

"He's young."

"And Douglas is old. Totally unattractive."

"He isn't old. A decade more than me: nothing."

"You're extremely well preserved. Tom would much rather be screwed by you; he told me that last night."

Oh, did he, I thought. I wouldn't mind that; I wouldn't mind it at all! Then a moment of disgust with myself, with the gay world: how do any of us manage to build friendships with other gay men? We're so competitive. Cock and arse are so often our driving needs, overruling affection, sympathy, support. We're all struggling against each other to get that chicken, that butch clone, and when we succeed we feel good. It's dehumanizing. Here I am being sorry for Nick because his lover is a whore, but I'll be in there with the lover if I've a chance. And probably hide the fact from Ulrich.

"Does this happen often?" I asked.

"Tom doing it with other men? Yes. All the time. And I'm monogamous. I haven't looked at anyone else since we met, haven't even wanted to. When he does this . . . I feel degraded. It's an insult. And a threat . . . I'm terrified that each one may be the start of a new, wonderful affair."

"Has that occurred? A suggestion of it occurring?"

"No. I have to admit that there's never been the slightest hint."

"Then . . . if you want to keep him, you have to put up with it."

"I don't know how long I can."

"You shouldn't say that! You seem . . . absolutely right for each other."

"We've had terrible rows. Why does he do it? I can't understand. Is my body ugly and boring, our sex life tediously predictable? No."

Why does he do it? Because he wants to assert his independence, be a free agent. His arse is his own property. See if he still can get a man. Ego boost. A change, another cock, is as good as a rest; maybe he likes to return to Nick reassured that no one else measures up. Nothing wrong in all that. And he wants the stability, the security of a long-term relationship. Nothing wrong in wanting that too. Nearly all of us need these supposed irreconcilables, and nearly all of us manage to reconcile them. Maybe Tom is more mature than Nick though ten years younger: Nick is the unstable, insecure partner.

"How do you and Ulrich cope?" he asked.

"We have other people from time to time, usually when one of us is away. We tell each other about it. The occasional threesome. It works. I don't think it *would* work if either of us insisted on monogamy."

"And would you tell him if you slept with Tom?"

This man is an emotional masochist, I said to myself: he's deliberately setting the situation up. "Probably not," I said. "For one reason: Ulrich is dying to have sex with you."

"I know."

"Maybe you ought to. I don't mind."

He shook his head. "I fancy him all right. But . . . I shan't."

"Tell me," I said, "how did Douglas get into your bed?"

"I couldn't sleep; that deck is so hard. I went for a walk, and when I returned I could see them at it. It was only an hour since he'd done it with me! So I came down here . . . I've been here all night."

"I think we should go back now," I said. The sun was up; there was traffic on the roads. Breakfast: I was starving.

All day the heat and heaviness built; clouds formed—we hadn't seen any for weeks—and swirled and frothed, grey, white, black, eventually blotting out the sun. There was tension in the sky, and on the boat: it was not a question of would there be a storm, but when. The humidity affected us all; we were listless, without energy. Even Martin. His promised "trip-ette" hurtling around on the open sea did not materialize, and I was thoroughly glad of that. We traveled much more slowly than we had done the previous evening, on Graham's insistence—he had appeared, full of the joys of spring, for breakfast; and at the same time Martin's chicken went off somewhere to his own breakfast. We anchored in a remote cove on the far side of Torbay. Nick swam to the beach and didn't come back till late afternoon; Tom lay in the powerboat's dinghy for hours, reading the Sunday papers. Douglas plowed on with his exam scripts. But Martin, Graham, Ulrich and I had a very pleasant time sprawled out nude on the deck, eating, drinking chilled white wine, and talking; not all of which was idle bragging of cocks and arses, or listening to tales of the speed of Martin's boat and the virtues of his other, multitudinous gadgets, or even gossiping about the problems in Nick's and Tom's relationship. We analyzed the government, a reasoned yet impassioned political argument; told stories of our parents, discussed films we had seen, swopped dinner recipes. Just four old friends chatting, our gayness not ignored, but for once not making us boast or compete.

Eventually the expected lightning flickered, then we heard a rumble of thunder so distant it could have been soft drum-taps. It was enough to galvanize Martin into action, however. "Come on, crew!" he shouted. "Anchors away!"

Tom swam from the dinghy, *The Observer* held high and dry above his head. "Wait for Nick," he said as he scrambled aboard. But Nick was swimming in our direction. I pulled him on to the boat: his face was black and ominous like the clouds.

"Don't do it here," I said.

"Don't do what here?" he panted, as he dried himself with a towel.

"Yell at Tom. One storm is enough to be getting on with."

He glared at me and turned away.

It was full steam ahead, probably wise on this occasion if we were to beat the weather. I lay in the cabin with Ulrich, on the bunk, as the boat dived and smacked to Torquay; it was as uncomfortable below deck as it had been yesterday up above. Several times we were levitated up into the air, then unceremoniously thrown back into the mattress. People drive these things at this speed for pleasure, I said to myself; it's incredible.

"I wonder what it would be like," Ulrich said, "to have sex while this is going on."

"Might be the last sex you'd ever have."

The full force of the storm hit us just after we had tied up in the marina. Lightning ripped the sky to shreds; thunder seemed to crack Torquay open, and the rain was a deluge, a wall of water. A moment before we left to dash to our cars, Tom, behind me as we climbed up the stairs from the cabin to the deck, said quietly, "When, David?"

I turned. "Whenever."

"I'll phone you."

"Come to my house tomorrow afternoon. Two o'clock."

He nodded. "O.K."

An enormous thrill of sexual desire rushed through me: lightning. His absolutely delicious young body.

"What was all that about?" Ulrich asked.

"Nothing," I answered.

Departures

for Matthias Daumann

D avid Crawshaw, you are just too soft with these people–"
"These people? These *people*! They're my *friends*, for Christ's sake!"
Ulrich folded his arms and breathed heavily. The blue eyes blazed.
"What's the use of me being your watchdog if you let the whole world into the house at all hours? Well? I try to keep them out, answer the phone for you, so you can write! You'll never get that book finished! You won't!"

"Yes I will."

"Now we Germans–"

"Ah yes, you Germans. Vays of making me verk." Ulrich looked severe. "You were meant to laugh," I said. "Or smile, at least."

"Ach, I give up." He stomped out of the room and went upstairs.

The reason for his bad temper was the chaos and confusion that Saturday morning; Andy, Phil, Martin, Pip and the next-door neighbors, Mr. and Mrs. Frumpitt, were all in the house. Andy would have been here anyway because he is our lodger. He's a cute young curly-haired blond, and an ideal tenant: undemanding, and he always pays the rent on time. He was off to Mykonos for a fortnight with Phil, his closest friend on our gay scene. Martin, who had now gotten his driving license back, was going to transport them to Heathrow; he was getting very obviously impatient while they rummaged through their suitcases; where was the Givenchy, the suntan lotion, the KY? And, oh my God! Phil's passport was missing. Then Pip arrived with a cat, an empty fish tank, and yogurt cartons full of glowering tropical fish: he was returning to London, so would I look after them? The fish, I mean, not the cat. Just for a couple of months, till he found a new place to live. The cat, christened Ms. (after me, he said) was apparently too ferocious a brute to leave with friends; she was being deposited, temporarily, with his married brother. Ms. evidently did not want to be deposited anywhere, for she shot under the sofa and scratched everyone who tried to wheedle her out.

"She's been in the trunk of my car," Pip explained.

"What a place to keep a cat!" Ulrich said.

"I don't *keep* her in the trunk. The back seat's piled high with luggage." The neighbors banged on the door. What were all those cars doing on the double yellow lines, Mr. Frumpitt wanted to know. It was illegal!

"Oh, is it really?" Andy said. But the sarcasm was lost on the Frumpitts. Pip grinned, and so did I. I had no time for our neighbors, who only spoke to us when they wanted to complain. "My wife's an old-aged pensioner, you know," Mr. Frumpitt was fond of telling us, as if this meant she had a divine right to more consideration than any other human being. "Yes," Ulrich once answered, "and we're all raving queens." Mr. Frumpitt didn't understand. "Militant lesbians," Ulrich went on, a remark which had useful consequences: our neighbors ignored us for the next six weeks.

"You can't leave cars outside here," Mr. Frumpitt said. "And there's three of them. *Three!*"

The house is in a narrow, pedestrianized street in Exeter's gay ghetto. Well...fourteen of us at the last head count; we like the little Victorian terraces in St. Matthew's and enjoy fixing them up as they do on Castro. Next year we're thinking of organizing the St. Matthew's Pride

March, just to show the natives we mean business and are here to stay. Martin's lover, Graham, will lead the procession dressed as a Sister of Perpetual Indulgence; Andy will appear as Tarzan with Robin as Jane; I'm going to be Elsie Tanner. Martin's idea, but he was drunk at the time and has probably forgotten all about it. I shan't remind him, as nothing on earth would induce me to wear drag; but I liked the comparison with Elsie Tanner. Quite a compliment: well worn and worn well.

"We shan't be long," Martin said to Mr. Frumpitt.

"Suppose an ambulance wants to get down the street?"

"In that case," said Phil, slowly, "I think. . .we'll move them."

Pip roared with laughter; Ms. scratched Ulrich: Andy said, "I can't find the KY anywhere; and Mr. Frumpitt left saying "I don't know. I don't know. I *really just don't know*!!"

"What doesn't he know?" Andy asked.

"The visible gay," I said. "The invisible kind I guess he can deal with."

At which point Ulrich took me into the kitchen to tell me I was too soft with my friends. His outburst was unusual, but there were tensions in our relationship. His job was moving back to London in a fortnight and we'd see each other only on weekends. Nothing we could do about that: but whereas I was philosophical, he found the idea of separation quite intolerable. "You can go to the baths every night," I said.

"I shan't."

"I bet you'll go occasionally."

"Will you sleep with other people when I'm away?"

"If they want to. And I want to. You'll do the same."

He sighed. "I expect so."

Actually, I didn't object to the thought of time on my own; I could get some work done. Ulrich was right: progress on the novel was at a snail's pace. But it wasn't, recently, friends dropping in that held me up so much as Ulrich himself, who, fearful of parting and worried at the loss of security, couldn't bear to spend one moment more than he had to away from me. So instead of writing the ultimate master-piece of the late twentieth century I seemed to find I was screwing.

Which was certainly not a waste of time: the best loving I've ever had, Ulrich, no doubt of that. But it didn't earn my bread and butter.

I knew, though, that the moment he'd gone I'd miss him, much as I told myself now that I needed his absence. I'd wander about the house sensing him in all the rooms, and yearn for Fridays when we'd meet, for the moment when I'd get his knickers off. And how long would that arrangement last? I've had experience before with a commuting lover. He soon met somebody else nearer to home.

"What's the matter with Ulrich?" Martin asked.

"Nothing important."

"He's always trying to take you away from us," Pip said. "I don't like it. At the disco last week he wouldn't let us near! I didn't dance with you at all that night! Which is unheard of."

"Pip is right," said Andy.

"Just a bit jealous," I told them.

"Jealous! He's got nothing to be jealous about."

"Leave it. Please." I was grateful for their affection; but embarrassed, for what they said was true.

"I must go," Pip said. He had succeeded in extricating Ms. from under the sofa. "Have a good holiday, you two. Mykonos! You'll be black from the sun, and knackered from all the fucking! God, how I envy you! And David. . .when you're in London, ring me. We'll have a meal and go to Harpoon Louie's and Heaven. *If* Ulrich lets you, that is."

"He will. Don't worry."

On the doorstep we all kissed, and waved goodbye. Take care, darling! Don't be good! 'Bye, honey! Don't *swish* like that! Send us a postcard! Pip, you're so *camp*! 'Bye! 'Bye!

The Frumpitts stood in their porch, glaring at us.

Back in the living room I noticed the fish tank. It was empty, and the fish were still struggling in their yogurt cartons. "The dizzy queen!" I said. "She hasn't put any water in the tank! Now what do we do?"

Phone calls all over the place, none of them suggesting where Pip might be. "Shove them in the kitchen sink," Andy said.

"I'm not having *anything* to do with this! If I'm to look after these monsters, he must give me some instructions!"

"The Frumpitts keep fish. Piranhas, I imagine. Ask them."

"I don't think I want to ask them anything."

"Maybe the Frumpitts are worried about property values," Martin said. "This house must be getting a bad reputation. *Must* be!"

I laughed, remembering something that had happened two weeks ago. "You know those friends of ours from Brighton who came to stay, Patrick and Chris? The guys who own the Green Carnation Hotel? Chris went out early one morning to buy a paper, then discovered he couldn't think of the number of our house. So he spoke to some old woman at the top of the street who was scrubbing her doorstep and asked her where we lived. She said she'd never heard of us, but it was number forty-nine if he wanted the house with the men."

"The house with the men. I like it!"

Another knock at the door: Pip, who'd left his glasses on the sofa in the battle with Ms. The fish he'd forgotten about. We reminded him. "Thank God I came back!" he said, and proceeded to rescue the unfortunate creatures from their yogurt-pot prisons.

Martin, Andy, and Phil were ready to leave at last, and the fish were swimming peacefully in their tank. More fond farewells outside: Andy promised to phone from Athens; Pip would send us all cards from Gay's the Word; Phil would bring me a gift-wrapped Greek god, and Martin said he'd see me and Ulrich at the gym.

The Frumpitts had gone indoors.

I stood, alone, in the living room: silence surged round me. I felt lost and sad. Then Ulrich came downstairs.

That evening we had dinner in the garden: salmon trout, white wine, a cherry and almond flan. Hot July weather. Scents of jasmine and honeysuckle; the distant noise of traffic. Summer night city. The air was velvet, mothy. We listened to the radio, Beethoven's Fourth Piano Concerto.

"The perfect music for a night like this," Ulrich said.

"I was just thinking that. Curious."

"What?"

"This concerto always reminds me of my mother."

"I thought you didn't like your mother."

"I don't."

Ulrich looked puzzled, but he didn't ask me to explain the paradox. I guess I couldn't have explained it. We sipped coffee, and sat in a warm silence. A bat flapped. "Shall we go down to Torquay?" he said.

"Yes." The club: friends, dancing, laughter, alcohol.

"Anything beforehand?"

On the bed, our naked bodies outlines in the dusk. What he wanted, as always, was what I wanted: he knew exactly the right moment I wanted to enter: and being inside him was still something to marvel at. Each time had the wonder of a first time. With how many other lovers have I experienced that feeling? None. The sweet preliminaries over, it was now a wild wrestling. One of these days, I thought, I'll hammer into him so far it will come out his ears.

We smoked cigarettes, our skin hot and sweaty, legs touching.

"Will it last?" he said.

"No. Nothing ever does."

Tears silently running down his face: I licked them dry. Then the sperm on his stomach. "What does it taste like?"

"Seaweed."

"Nice?"

"Yes."

"It will last."

"Don't spoil it. Think of now."

"I'm erect."

"You always are."

"Are you?"

"No. But with a little coaxing. . ."

"I'll coax it." His fingers, brushing the hair between my legs. "It didn't need much persuasion."

"For you it's a mile high in ten seconds."

I thought, as we made love again, of the road to Torquay, the trees of Exeter Forest flashing by in the dark. The gentle deer that some-times froze in the headbeams: the sea not so far off, down to our left, whispering to itself. The city lights behind us. Shakatak on the cassette: *Nightbirds, Easier Said than Done:* Ahead, the club: our friends—Graham and Brian and Steven and Kevin and Robin and Alex and Mark.

Hot summer nights. Halcyon. Being gay in the remote provinces, and happy.

Gay Cat Burglar Seeks Same for Long-Lasting Relationship

To whom it may concern:

You will have to bear with the writer of this little morality tale when you come to the first juicy bit; it's a heterosexual coupling. However, everything comes to him who waits, though I have doubts about whether you will ever read this story: I'm writing it in prison, on sheets of toilet paper, and I shall have to find some way of smuggling them out.

I'm a cat burglar by profession, and a pretty good one—I've never been caught. It's a difficult and dangerous line of work, as you can easily imagine, requiring strength, agility and coordination; coolness and precise attention to detail; and a capacity for making lightning-quick decisions. I used to keep fit by lifting weights in a gym, and at the time of these events I had superb biceps, chest muscles and legs. My mind, too, was sharp and experienced. But there's always a weakness, a flaw in the pattern, and mine was an insatiable appetite for sleeping with beautiful girls—the more I had the more I wanted.

Perhaps it seems unlikely that sex should be the undoing of a cat burglar, but in my case it was so. I made two other mistakes that night, but they were not important, not instrumental in bringing my career to an end. One was that the moonlight was more brilliant than I had anticipated, and the second error was that the bedroom into which I climbed—with great ease; it was the hottest night of the summer and the window was open—did not contain the old lady I had observed through a pair of powerful binoculars the week before. A young woman lay on the bed, stark naked. (The sheet had presumably been thrown off because of the heat.) She had gorgeous big breasts and her legs were wide open. I suppose I might just about have been able to ignore this and get on with my job, except for the fact that she was obviously dreaming. Obvious, too, was the nature of her dream; the quick breathing and the little moans that escaped her lips were not the noises of nightmare.

I watched, fascinated, with an erection two miles high. Her breathing became hoarse, and she wriggled slightly. I couldn't stop myself: my fingers were touching the skin above her left breast. "Damian," she murmured. Soon my hand was on the breast itself; then my tongue gently sliding over the nipple, and—absolute madness!—I was unzipping my jeans, pushing them down my legs. " 'Slovely, lovely," she whispered. I was naked, stroking her, stroking her—this could not be wham, bang, over and done with in five minutes; it would have to be quieter and more controlled than anything I'd done before. I made a mental note of exactly where I'd left my clothes in case I had to run for my life.

Penetration incredibly slow. Then I started. No doubt of it, one of the most delicious fucks I'd ever had. There's a lot to be said, I thought, for infinite patience and gentleness in sex. "Damian, this is the best!" she whispered. "And you feel. . .different, somehow. Bigger. Better." She was now awake, but probably had not opened her eyes: I couldn't tell, as I'd deliberately positioned my head with the moonlight behind it so my face would be in shadows, and it meant I couldn't see her face, either. Nice to know I was better than Damian. And bigger. Well . . . I was first in line when those were given out. She began to climax, but I'm not going to describe it: this story is for gay readers.

The perfection of my own orgasm was my downfall. Control had gone; the noises I was making were, I imagine, quite different from her boyfriend's little whimpers, for she suddenly went rigid and said, "You're not Damian!" I was out of her and off the mattress all in one movement. I was zipping up my jeans when she snapped on the bedside light. In those split seconds we took a mental photograph of each other we'd probably remember for the rest of our days—I of an expression of incredulity and terror; she of a young man with long blond hair, big biceps and piercing blue eyes.

She began to scream at the top of her voice. I jumped out of the window, landed on some flowers, and fled through the garden. She was at the window, yelling "Rape! Rape! Rape!" It wasn't rape, I told myself. False pretences, yes, but surely mutual pleasure: "Damian, this is the best!" But it was a line of reasoning the judge at my trial refused to take into consideration.

In the street I collided with a cop, who was running towards the house, because I guess, he had heard the woman's screams. He was winded by the impact and stumbled; I was able to sprint across the road and down a side alley before he could recover. But I soon heard his footsteps, and a shout of "Stop! I'll fire!" The only refuge this little street offered was an open, ill-lit doorway. I dashed inside, just as he turned the corner, and heaved a sigh of relief—he ran on past. Where was I? When I realized what this building was used for—why, at one a.m., it was open—I began to count my blessings. It was an almost perfect hide-out: I was in a gay bathhouse.

Perfect, because mingling with a couple of hundred men who were all dressed in nothing but brief towels round their waists would give me an anonymity I never could have wearing clothes. I hadn't been in such an establishment before, and I didn't know what to expect, but I assumed that politely declining any sexual overture would not be taken amiss—the man concerned would merely think he wasn't my type and go on to look for somebody else. I didn't exactly relish the idea of being importuned, but that was a small matter compared with being arrested on a charge of rape. I handed over my entrance fee, found a cubicle and shut myself inside it; then undressed, and lay down on the bed. The police might raid the place in their search for me, but there were, I had noticed when I walked from the desk to my cubicle, plenty of other blue-eyed blonds. In the dim lighting of the bathhouse identification would be difficult. Anyway, since the gay population started to get militant ten or fifteen years ago, the police don't like to burst into bathhouses and round up faggots—rocks have been thrown at them and their cars fire-bombed. I had also observed that there was a veritable rabbit warren of dark passageways, up and down which the clientele stalked one another, a network of corridors so complex it would be relatively easy to elude the police—even supposing they had guessed I was in here, which wasn't absolutely certain.

How long should I stay, I wondered. All night, perhaps—it would be safer to go when it was daylight and I could mix with other people in the streets. Alone, at four o'clock in the morning is automatically suspicious. Maybe I could sleep—the little bed was quite comfortable. But I was tense after what had happened, and there was too much noise—loud music, and the moans and groans of orgasms in the adjacent cubicles. I began to get bored.

Very bored.

I could wander about and see what was happening. It would be instructive, and I didn't have to join in. What I would see wouldn't disgust me, I guessed. I have, in fact, had sex with another male, a Puerto Rican boy, ten years ago when I was fourteen. We did it several times over a period of about six months—it was mostly just a fun thing, jacking each other off, trying to shoot the furthest; but I have to admit I was occasionally more serious than that. He had a slim, feminine body, and at times I enjoyed doing it, naked, lying on top of him. I even liked kissing him. I was fond of that kid—but it all stopped about the time of my fifteenth birthday, when I began to screw girls.

I stood on the bed and peered over the wall into the next cubicle, but it was too dark to see much—just the silhouettes of writhing bodies. So I unlocked the door and ventured out.

Quite an eye-opener. My reaction, ultimately, was that it's a great pity a straight equivalent of the bathhouse syndrome does not exist.

If it did, I think I'd be in there every night of the week. Our nearest thing, I suppose, is a brothel, but with a whore you can pay the earth for a tenth-rate mechanical fuck. In the bathhouse you pay to get in, certainly, but after that you have choice—a vast range of choices that are free, and I imagine much of the pleasure is experimenting for a while with this one and that one, and if he doesn't measure up to what you really want you move around till you find the one who does. The variety of experiences on offer makes me envious—gays have much more than straights! You can spend hours here with just one guy, or come with several different men. You can fuck or get fucked, suck or get sucked; indulge in mutual masturbation, have three-ways, group sex—I watched couples on beds, a dozen guys enjoying an orgy, two cocks inside one ass at the same time, guys looking at skin flicks and jacking off alone, cocks through holes in walls being sucked by mouths the cock's owner never saw. Straight sex, after this, even if it was preferable and more satisfying for me, seemed somewhat limited in what could or could not be done.

The place was immaculate, deluxe—showers, steam room, dry sauna, and a hot tub as big as a Roman bath. I lay in the hot tub and thought about it all.

I still wasn't tired. Nor did I want to join in—but the sight of all those people uninhibitedly enjoying each other's bodies made me not just envious, but wanting sex. How? After ages of saying no, no, no to myself, I stuck my cock through one of those anonymous holes. A tongue on the other side licked. It felt good, and my cock soon swelled to its normal size. An unseen mouth is an unseen mouth—it couldn't really matter that it wasn't female when it was impossible to see whose it was. I imagined Damian's girl's lips and tongue. Just before orgasm I pulled away. I like being sucked, but it's an unsatisfactory way of coming: your cock doesn't have the usual tight tunnel wrapped delectably round it.

What now? Bring myself off, I suppose. But that was unsatisfactory too. I knew exactly what I wanted, but I couldn't get it in here, of course. There was one obvious substitute, but did I really want to do that? And if I did, how would I regard myself afterwards? It took a long time to decide that I wouldn't find any serious dents in my image—then even longer to pick someone with whom I thought I'd enjoy it.

My choice—not so surprising, I guess—was the only Puerto Rican in the place, slim and girlish, smooth-chested and young, like that kid of years ago. I didn't know if he would do what I wanted—one odd aspect of the bathhouse ritual, I noticed, is that despite all the intimacy between body and body hardly anyone speaks to anyone else—but I was reassured when we went to his cubicle and he lay on his back, legs wide apart. "I've got some KY," he said—his first words to me. So, with my cock and his ass well lubricated, I pushed at his knees till they were resting on his shoulders, his ass therefore a few inches up from the bed, and prised myself in. It was immensely more satisfying than I had imagined—tight, slippery, my cock really deep inside. Orgasm was fantastic.

I had thought I'd be out of that room as soon as it was over, but here I was holding him in my arms, panting, exhausted. And half an hour later at it again. Wild, uninhibited fucking this time, and twisting his tits till he moaned with pleasurable pain. So often with women I'd wanted to inflict pain but never had, and here was this guy saying, "At home I've got nipple clamps, handcuffs! I love being tied up and beaten with a leather strap!"

"And I'd love to do it to you," I said. Though he wasn't ready himself, I couldn't hold back my orgasm any longer.

When I'd subsided, emerged, he said "Suck me off." Oh, why not? First time I'd ever had a cock in my mouth and tasted semen. Didn't exactly do much for me, but, once again, I wasn't disgusted. Gay men, I began to realize, constantly have to put up with heterosexual images—men and women kissing in the streets and the parks; in movies, making love—and they probably aren't revolted at the sight. Many of them may have slept with girls before they had the courage to do what they really wanted to do. I doubt if they are disgusted—just indifferent. Perhaps, I began to think, straights could learn quite a bit, liberate themselves, by studying gay life-styles and attitudes.

"I'm tired," I said.

"Let's sleep. Curl up round me. I like that." I did so. It was tender, intimate.

I woke, hours later, to find him standing by the bed, staring down at me. He had his clothes on. I couldn't move my arms; they were behind my back: I was handcuffed. "What the hell's going on?" I said.

"You're under arrest."

"Arrest? What for?"

"What do you think? I'm the cop you slammed into. Oh yes, I saw you come in here, so I knew I didn't need to hurry. Nobody ever comes in here for less than three or four hours. I had plenty of time to take a statement from the girl, then go back and file my report, shower, change, and get ready for the tubs. As a *duty*. I've never been able to do that. Could I claim it as expenses? Hmmmm. . .perhaps not. O.K.. . .it's years in the pen for you. Get your jeans on."

"I can't if I'm in handcuffs."

"I'll unlock them. Don't do anything crazy—I've still got my gun." He held it in one hand as I dressed, and fondled my cock with the other. "That's a mighty efficient weapon," he said. "You certainly know what to do with it. You'll enjoy yourself in jail."

"You're going to look pretty dumb when I tell the judge what happened tonight."

"The cop who arrested you let you fuck him twice before he produced the handcuffs? In a gay bathhouse? With you on a charge of raping a *woman*? Do you really think anyone's going to believe you?"

I had no answer to that—he was absolutely right. "I did not rape her," I said.

"What were you doing in her bedroom then?" I *could* not answer that. "One thing puzzles me," he said. "You fuck a woman once, then fuck a man twice. All in the space of four or five hours. Seems to me you're a bit. . .kinky. But I've never been able to understand bisexuals."

"I'm not bisexual."

"Oh?"

"And I'm not gay, either."

He laughed. "Married with two-point-four children and a mortgage, I suppose; neat little house in Milpitas?"

"Not exactly."

"Well, what exactly? What *were* you doing in her bedroom? Burglary?"

I refused to answer that.

Which is why I'm in the clink for a crime I did not commit. I will never agree that I raped her; I've never hurt anybody in my life except in my fantasies. But I'm going to. One of the first things I shall do when I get out of here is track down that cop and break into his apartment. He said he liked being tied up and beaten with a leather strap. I'll tie him up all right! And I'll give him the beating of his life. There won't be much left of his buns when I've finished with them. If he can walk after six months I'll be amazed. And while he's bound and gagged, I shall steal every valuable object that he owns.

Prison is absolutely awful. Much, much worse than anything I could have dreamed in my most horrifying nightmares. I'm all in favor of that program showing young delinquents what it's really like inside — you know, taking them to the pokey and letting them see for themselves. It soon puts them off a life of crime. And don't believe a word those old right-wing blue-rinsed ladies tell you about jails — that we have all the luxuries we could want, that conditions are so much better than in the outside world we'd prefer to stay in. It's a 100 percent gigantic lie. Perhaps you think I should have told the truth about being a burglar, that it might have led to the rape charge being dropped, or questioned at least. Burglary often gets a lighter sentence. The point is I have to have something to fall back on when I'm out of here. The loot. The money in my bank account. And a return to the old profession — as I said, I've never been caught.

There's only one good thing about prison — my cell-mate. An attractive young Vietnamese, slim, boyish, etcetera. He chopped his father up with an axe; in self-defense, he says. It's difficult to imagine — he's a waif, in need of love, care and protection. So I protect him — from the other prisoners. They'd all like to get their cocks between his cute little buns, which I may say provide me with an exquisite fuck every day of the week. My sex life is just as good as it was when I was a free man.

I'll be out soon, and I'm beginning to think a bit more about the future. No reason, as I said, why I shouldn't go back to the old profession. I'll stay gay, however—I've gotten so used to it and enjoy it so much I don't think women would do a lot for me. I'd like to settle down, now I'm in my thirties. With another man as my lover, someone who's also in the profession—it would be awkward if he was a librarian or an attorney or a schoolteacher. I think I'll put an advertisement in the *Village Voice* or the *Bay Area Reporter*: "Good-looking, extremely well-hung, blond, blue-eyed, six feet, one fifty pounds, gay male seeks, for long-lasting relationship, attractive young gay cat burglar who's into being fucked."

All letters will be answered, and don't worry about stamped, addressed envelopes; I'll pay the postage. I can afford it.

Quiet Days in Los Gatos

for Marian Robinson

J ack fell in love with the house the moment he saw it. A long, low, L-shaped structure, half-hidden by cypress and persimmon trees; the garden, which had a swimming pool, so filled with flowering shrubs he could not discern its edges let alone the neighbors' roofs. Bees swarmed, busy in the myrtle blossom. A stone's throw away it seemed the Santa Cruz mountains occupied half the sky: gentle, rolling summits parched brown and ochre by the summer sun.

Inside was dark after the dazzling August light; the living room, spacious, untidy with hundreds of books, was the center of the house, the joining of the two parts of the letter L. At one extremity was the huge room where Harriet slept and lived for most of the time, a converted garage he was told; at the other, beyond the kitchen and the spare bedrooms and bathrooms, was the room he could rent. Old oak furniture – family heirlooms perhaps – and a double bed; French windows that opened on to a veranda and which could be his private entrance if he wanted. His own bathroom. A view of the swimming pool, the mountains; sun on green leaves.

Aaron had discovered it. He knew the two women slightly—friends of friends of friends. "They're lesbians," he said, when Jack, on hearing the older woman, Harriet, had four grown-up children, asked if she was a widow and simply sharing with a friend; "do you think I'd dump you on to some straight ménage?" It wasn't exactly the kind of place Jack had thought, beforehand, that he'd be living in; a room not too far from Castro, in an urban house with half a dozen other gay men, had seemed the obvious choice, despite the fifty mile commute to work. Here, in Los Gatos, he would be only a short drive from his teaching job in San José, a city, Aaron said, that had a few gay bars, and he could always come up to San Francisco at week-ends. "San José has the Watergarden," he added.

"What is the Watergarden?" Jack asked.

"The best baths in California. Full of delectable Vietnamese boys . . . so Luke tells me."

On that first visit to Los Gatos, Sarah was not at home. Harriet perched on the red settee in the living room, drinking beer in the late afternoon, evidently trying to sum up the character of her prospective tenant. She was about fifty, Jack guessed, slim, with grey hair, unfashionably dressed; her face lined—prematurely, he imagined, because of the eternal sun—and her dark eyes were narrow slits like the spaces between drawn curtains.

"I hope Aaron told you I'm gay," he said.

"Yes. It makes no difference."

Her answer sounded odd, but it was only later that he said to himself he'd expected her to feel more, not less, comfortable with a gay tenant. They agreed about the rent, and, at Jack's insistence, that he would cook his own meals. "But eat with us when you want to," Harriet said. He liked the idea of the French windows as his own front door: less awkward if he brought a man home for the night. He could move in on Sunday.

As he drove away he wondered why Sarah had not been there. Wouldn't she, too, want to size up the new lodger? Harriet had behaved as if Sarah's opinion was of no significance. He thought perhaps the room that would be his might in fact be Sarah's; that she had been turned out of it to make space for him. But he dismissed his uneasy feelings: the house was beautiful, the garden and the surrounding countryside perfect; he was twenty minutes from work and the Watergarden sounded interesting, just right—he was in no frame of mind to start an affair, but he needed sex of course. He could be absolutely private at Los Gatos, unlike the multiple living of a gay city tenement—the noise of other people's radios, the smells of their cooking, queuing up to use a shared, grubby bathroom. He could be happy.

It seemed to work very well. Sarah, if she had indeed been made to give up her room, showed no hostility; she was the more relaxing of the two to be with—large, motherly, and outgoing. Harriet was less easy to define. Quick-witted, amusing, but . . . secretive? Was that the right word? The day he moved in they ate together—Sarah cooked—and drank a lot of wine, then told each other their biographies. "It's good to have a past to relate," Jack said.

"I've no interest in the young," Harriet said. "They know nothing and they learn nothing."

"Don't you find any of them . . . sexually attractive?"

"Gay people are obsessed with sexual attraction!"

"You're gay."

"No, I'm not." She laughed. "And I don't usually like gay men."

"Why not?"

"It means a few less men in the world for me! But you're different. You've got good vibes. I never think of myself as gay. Sarah is."

"Though we've lived together for eighteen years," said Sarah. She went out to the kitchen to make coffee and do the dishes.

"People are people," Harriet said. "Does it matter what gender they are?"

"I've never fancied a woman," Jack said. "I've never slept with a woman."

"I find that quite extraordinary! How old are you? Thirty?"

"Almost."

"I'm sure everyone is capable of loving either sex."

"Yes. *Making* love . . . no."

"When I was engaged to be married, I went on vacation once with a girl friend. Oh, an old friend from school days . . . we knew each other very well. We were sharing the same room . . . . One night . . . I realised I wanted to go to bed with her. In the morning I was terrified by what we'd done! I called my fiancé and said let's get married at once!"

"And did you?"

"Yes."

"Which turned out to be a mistake?"

"No, no. I was very happy having lots of children. We divorced eventually, but that wasn't a result of me liking women. Then I met Sarah."

"And you lived happily ever after?"

"I wouldn't put it precisely like that," said Sarah, returning with the coffee.

But alone with Jack, Sarah showed no tartness. They walked up in the hills, taking her dog with them, and discussed books, politics, people, religion; it was all very amicable. She said nothing on any occasion that suggested life with Harriet was less than perfect. But their existence together was strange, Jack thought, eccentric even. They did not demonstrate their affection for one another, not even by a touch of the hand or a shared smile. The living room was merely a space to walk through; that first visit to the house was the only time he ever saw Harriet sitting there. They both worked during the day—they were professors at San José University—and in the evening they would eat in the kitchen and talk of this and that for maybe an hour, then retire to separate parts of the house, Harriet to her converted garage, Sarah to one of the other bedrooms. There they would read or prepare lectures every night, including weekends. They were workaholics: never went out, never entertained, spent no time together apart from the hour of the evening meal, didn't watch television, listen to music, or break off occasionally to speak to each other. It was weird, he thought; surely if you and your partner of eighteen years both wanted to read books you could enjoy doing so in one room, not two. He suspected that on many nights they did not sleep in the same bed; he even began to doubt Aaron's information—they behaved like roommates, not lovers.

Jack came and went as he pleased. He, too, had to work some evenings of the week—texts to prepare, papers to mark. On other nights the Watergarden proved much as Aaron had said; he usually left it having had some exhilarating experience. Or experiences. Aaron's "delectable" wasn't exactly the right word to describe screwing with a Vietnamese, but it was certainly very satisfactory—they were athletic, sensual: expert. Best sex I've had in years, he thought. On Friday afternoons he went to San Francisco and stayed till Sunday, usually at Aaron's house, spending his time at concerts, the theatre, sampling the pleasures Castro had to offer or just strolling about the streets enjoying the beauty of the place.

He had settled into a new life with an ease that surprised him.

About two months after he moved to Los Gatos, Harriet asked him to dinner; they had bought, she said, a leg of lamb much too big for her and Sarah to eat alone. Once again a large quantity of wine was drunk, and what they talked about was the same as on the last occasion— Harriet's inability to understand that there could be people who were exclusively interested in one or the other sex. It was also, as before, a conversation in which Sarah did not participate much. Shortly after midnight, when Jack discovered that the alcohol had gone to his head, and that he had probably been talking nonsense for the past half hour— babbling away about Kevin's shabby, underhanded actions during the break-up of their nine year affair—he realized Sarah was no longer in the house, had not in fact been there for some time.

"Where is she?" he asked.

"Sarah? Gone to bed, I guess," Harriet said. "Or out for a walk maybe."

"I must go to bed too." He looked at his watch. "I'm drunk; it's late, and I have to teach in a few hours' time."

He was just dozing off when someone knocked on his door. He got up, walked across the room and switched on the light. "Who is it?" he called, sleepily.

Harriet came in, not waiting to be asked. But I'm naked, he thought, as he quickly hurried back under the sheet. And semi-erect. "Is Sarah in here?"

"Sarah! Of course not!"

"Are you sure?"

"Do you think she's lurking in the closet or something?"

"I'm sorry . . . I can't find her anywhere."

She left. What on earth was she up to? She looked at me . . . She wants *my* body? It was ludicrous. He pushed the idea out of his head and fell asleep.

In the morning neither woman made any reference to the previous night. Jack walked up in the hills for an hour with Sarah and the dog, and their conversation was almost entirely about movies. This piece of landscape appealed to him very much; he felt he had grown into it, or it had become part of him. Why it should be important and so suddenly important puzzled him, as if the scenery of the rest of his life, London, the estuary, the Devon moors, were of little account now. He was not homesick, and astonished that he was not. He had already come to regard Los Gatos as home. Its buildings stopped only a hundred yards from the house and the road petered out in the derelict, overgrown grounds of a monastery: neglected vineyards occupying the whole of a steep hillside, unpruned peach trees, withered grass where a few horses tried to forage, olive trees from which the crop had fallen and been crushed underfoot. Fennel grew in cracks in the unused road, its pungent scent drifting on the wind. Beyond the monastery grounds the mountain trails led through woods of eucalyptus, oak and poison oak, across dried up streams and waterfalls, eventually to bare uplands of brown grass and dust. Dust everywhere—it was October and there had been no rain since March. It did not seem possible to Jack that it would ever rain again. At dusk, the Santa Clara Mountains on the far side of San José seemed incandescent, to glow, as if they were releasing the heat that punished and penetrated them all day long; they were burnished, like bronze or brass.

"It does rain," Sarah said. "In winter you'll be surprised how green it is. As green as England."

"I want it to be sunshine always!" Jack said. "I love it!" Ninety degrees or more every day, a dry heat that was rarely troublesome, though it was October and the light had begun to slant, had the gold color of fall. He looked good—slimmer, fitter, skin superbly tanned, hair bleached white by the sun. Looking as he did, he never had any trouble finding sex.

He loved the views from the summits. The vast sprawl of San José filled the plain below, but it was so well planted with trees that most of its buildings, its dreary estates of houses and factories, were hidden. Downtown was often lost in smog. One structure, resembling a Greek temple, always stood out. It was probably a bank. The Santa Clara Mountains were stark and bare, moon mountains, barren, treeless, their outlines and folds like a model of hills in grey clay. Though people tell you it's a mini Los Angeles it's just like modern Athens, he thought—a hideous, smoggy city in a beautiful, ancient landscape.

"How do you like living with two women?" Sarah asked.

"Fine. Just fine." Though it would be easier with men, more intimacy, more . . . shared assumptions. He wouldn't, for example, feel he ought not to bring a man home for sex; it would be considered odd if he didn't.

"Do you know many gay women in Britain?"

"No. A pity, really." Was it? Almost all the lesbians he'd met, or heard about, were strident, quarrelsome and aggressive, living up to the stereotypical image of diesel dykes brandishing spanners. Fat arses squashed into jeans. They were often as homophobic in their attitudes to gay men as were Norman Normals from Neasden.

"Lesbians have yet to make themselves visible," Sarah said. "When we do—then watch out, world!"

Jack laughed. "Will you be with them?"

She wrinkled her nose, a gesture of mild disgust. "I've never even marched in the San Francisco Gay Freedom Day Parade. Yet."

These two weren't like the stereotypes he knew, he said to himself.

When they returned to the house, Harriet was in the garden talking to a man. A large battered suitcase, evidently full of possessions, stood just inside the gate. Sarah froze. "That's Konstantin," she said.

"Who's he?"

"Some bit of stuff she picked up on vacation in Greece last year."

"Konstantin is staying for a week," Harriet said. "Isn't that nice?" A dark-skinned man, Jack noticed, very hairy, with piercing blue eyes.

At a Hallowe'en party in San Francisco he met a man called Richard. Every weekend after that was spent in his company, though Jack continued to see Luke and Aaron. They knew Richard, and liked him. Jack went less frequently to the Watergarden, but he didn't stop going altogether. "I don't see why I should do without it," he said. "It's a different kind of experience."

"There are worse things in life to cope with than sexual jealousy," said Sarah as she downed her fifth brandy. "You don't own someone else's body. Or so I try to tell myself."

"I tried to tell myself that too," Jack answered. "Once upon a time. I believed it; I believe it still . . . but it isn't exactly an instant cure."

"I was going to spend the evening reading Virginia Woolf. But I think I'd see the pages double."

"Have another brandy. Go on. help yourself."

She poured two and handed one to him, very unsteadily. "Have you read *Mrs. Dalloway?*" she asked.

"Yes."

"Do you think it's all transmuted autobiography?"

"How can she bring him here to the house with you here . . . it's *inhuman!* Even Kevin didn't do such things. Behind my back, yes, but only when he knew I wasn't at home. Why, if she has to sleep with him, can't she do so without you knowing anything about it? Visit him in some hotel room in San José."

"I'd rather discuss Virginia Woolf. It's less squalid."

"O.K."

"Well . . . a week is soon gone."

"Harold Wilson, one of our better prime ministers, said a week in politics was a long time. With sexual jealousy, I guess a week is a *very* long time."

"There's no need for you to worry yourself about any of it."

It wasn't worry; it was . . . discomfort. Konstantin, a fawn-like man, delicate on the surface but as hard as nails underneath, was quite amiable, but Jack found it almost impossible to respond to his small talk. They went up into the mountains one afternoon; his replies to Konstantin's chatter were monosyallables. He is polluting my landscape, he said to himself, though he realized the moment the words entered his mind that they were absurd. This Greek guy is Pan, he thought, the goat-god, lecherous as a goat. He remembered his comparison of San José to modern Athens. Didn't Pan belong to such a landscape? Anyway . . . why should he care that Konstantin was upsetting Sarah? She was over forty, hardly a child in need of his protection. She had choice, could take a dozen or more courses of action.

It was for himself that he was disturbed. The neat arrangements of his life, the mix of the placid, soothing household was changed, maybe permanently. Harriet, when she thought about it, would probably not like what she'd allowed him to see. She'd make trouble. He could always move in with Richard, he supposed, but he wasn't sure that would work. The week in rural Los Gatos, Friday to Sunday in the whirl of San Francisco, the occasional exciting hunt for an Oriental body, made a perfectly balanced existence. He didn't want any kind of change.

The day after Konstantin left he arrived home from a vigorous, indeed very rough session at the Watergarden, his body satiated with exertion as if he'd spent long hours at a gym. He felt utterly at peace with the world. The house stood well back from the road, but he could hear the yelling before he turned into the drive and parked his car. The curtains were not drawn in Harriet's room; she was sitting on the bed, quite still, while Sarah shrieked at her and hurled saucepans, ornaments and books. He hurried away and walked for a while in the monastery grounds, listening to night noises—the bleep-bleep-bleep of thousands of crickets, distant dogs barking, the shrill protest of a jay woken from slumber. He crept back in through his French windows. All the lights were out. Absolute silence. "I WILL NOT PUT UP WITH IT ANY MORE!" Sarah had screamed. "ONE AFTER ANOTHER! YEAR AFTER YEAR! SHARON!"—saucepan crashing into the bedside lamp—"CHUCK!"—books flung at random—"ANNE-MARIE!"—statuette of a naked woman aimed directly at Harriet, who dodged just in time—"KARL!"—kettle whizzing through the air—"SOPHIE!"—an encyclopedia narrowly missing a window—"KON-STAN-TIIINNN!!!—and a huge casserole dish wrecked the picture over the bed, scattering splinters of glass in all directions.

Male and female alternately, he said to himself as he undressed. Was I supposed to act out some part in this charade? Konstantin instead, when she knew I wouldn't? She won't admit that for me it's men only. She eventually came to the conclusion—or will eventually come to the conclusion—that I simply don't want her: an insult, she'll decide, rather than a good reason. No . . . nonsense. There isn't any evidence that shows she fancies me at all. I'm just the tenant. Thank God.

At dinner next day Harriet and Sarah were friendly, with Jack as well as with each other. Harriet was a bit subdued, but there was no other sign that anything out of the ordinary had happened. Maybe it wasn't out of the ordinary, Jack thought; it could be an experience they went through from time to time, that had certain conventions and well-defined limits, which left the relationship in a better state than it had been in previously. It was possible. After a week, Harriet's humor was quite restored. Over a cocktail one evening she said the reason why one never saw any monks up at the monastery was that they were permanently smashed out of their tiny heads; since eighteen something or other they had managed to turn the wine their grapes produced from a totally disgusting brew that tasted like urine into one that was extremely bad, but just about drinkable if you were already high on something else. They were always suffering from king-size hangovers; "a monk as drunk as a skunk," she said.

These humorous anecdotes only came when she was in the best of moods. The name Los Gatos—Spanish for "the cats"—was not, as the guide-books said, because of the stone cats in the driveway of the oldest house in town, but because in the gold rush years the prospectors needed their women, so just down the road from here they built the biggest cat-house in the West.

"But there were no gold mines in the Santa Cruz Mountains," Jack said.

"Oh . . . there must have been some," she said, vaguely. "Otherwise why put an enormous brothel here? On the San Andreas Fault, too."

"Don't ask practical questions," Sarah said. "It spoils the game. It breaks the rules."

Harriet laughed, and poured herself another vodka.

"I see," Jack said. "Placing it on the San Andreas was silly; you're quite right. When it was packed on a Saturday evening all that thrust and shove could have caused an earthquake."

Harriet's eyes shone. "It did, it did! That's precisely what happened! How clever of you to guess!"

Sarah smiled. She looked happy and relaxed.

Later, when he was in bed, he heard them swimming in the pool. Midnight, and pitch dark. They really were a crazy pair, he thought with amusement and affection. But he decided not to look out of the window: their nakedness did not appeal.

"Haven't you any classes to teach today?" Harriet said one morning.

"Of course. I'm just leaving."

"Good," she answered. "Good!"

What now, he asked himself as he drove into San José. He had seen little of her during the past week, and, he realized, when they had spoken she'd been somewhat distant. No jokes about monks or whore houses, indeed anything. Did she feel his air of moral superiority over the Konstantin business had been insufferable? What had Sarah told her? It was a very hot day, a scorcher. When he returned from school, he took off his clothes and went into the garden in swimming trunks. Harriet was working by the poolside. "Hi," he said.

"Hi," she answered, without looking up, then shuffled her papers together and disappeared into the house. The same thing happened the following afternoon. He had just lit a cigarette. "I can't stand your filthy smoke," she said. "It makes me puke!" She was yards away; she couldn't possibly have smelled it. She had said when Jack first rented the room that she had an allergy to cigarettes and had asked him not to smoke in the house, except in his own room. Or the garden, she added; of course it was O.K. in the garden. But she'd often told him subsequently, when they ate together or had a drink and he'd said he'd go outside for a drag, that he didn't have to; it would not bother her in the least. Her allergy, he concluded, was neither physical nor psychological—it was a weapon. He dove into the pool and splashed about enjoyably for half an hour. As he walked to his room, dripping wet, hair plastered to his scalp, he saw her watching from her bedroom window.

The morning paper, usually left in the kitchen for him to read, was never in evidence now. She took it to her room, and as he didn't like to go in and borrow it when she wasn't there—or indeed to ask for it when she *was* there—he knew little of what was happening in the world. He could have ordered his own paper of course, but that would have been absurd—two copies of *The San Francisco Chronicle* in a house-hold of three. She removed the television from the living room and put it beside her bed—not that its loss bothered him any more than the disappearance of the newspaper; he was not a TV addict even in Britain where there were, in his opinion, at least *some* programs worth watching. It was the sheer pettiness of the harassments that angered him, as indeed they were meant to; the deliberate avoidance of any direct comment. She must be enjoying her silly little games immensely, he said to himself. In the first cold days of winter—it was three weeks before Christmas—Harriet lit the stove in her room and a huge fire of logs blazed, but she said nothing about how he was supposed to keep himself warm in his part of the house.

"I've just paid her the rent," he said to Sarah. "Two hundred and fifty dollars a month, for which I don't, it seems, get any heating!"

"There's an electric heater in one of the closets. I'll go find it for you."

"What is the matter with her? What am I supposed to have done to make her behave like this?"

Sarah put down the erudite tome on the Bloomburys that she was reading, took off her glasses, and smiled. "It's nothing you've *done*," she said.

"What do you mean?"

"It's . . . well, maybe who you are . . . what you are . . . "

"Why doesn't she come right out with it?"

Sarah laughed. "That is never Harriet's method. Never!"

"I don't understand your riddles."

"Maybe it's something . . . you *haven't* done."

"It's all extremely unpleasant," Jack said. "If she doesn't treat me a little better, I shall look for somewhere else to live."

This, he knew, was an idle threat. His room, the garden, the walks in the hills, the privacy, the quiet—these were the stable planks of his life; not more than his job, the Watergarden, or the San Francisco weekends with Richard, but the house in Los Gatos was central to his present equilibrium. He hoped Sarah would tell Harriet of the conversation they had just had, so that something could be said to clear the air.

When he returned from San Francisco the Sunday evening before Christmas he was surprised to find the house in darkness. Gone to bed very early, he said to himself as he moved quietly about the kitchen, making a cup of tea. I wish they all could be California girls, he hummed under his breath; I mean boys. Harriet's door, he noticed, was open.

Footsteps. She was wearing a red dressing gown. "What are you doing creating a racket in the middle of the night?" she demanded.

He sipped his tea and looked at her. "It is not the middle of the night," he said, "and I am not creating a racket."

"I was asleep. You woke me up."

A lie; he knew that. "Why don't you shut your bedroom door? You wouldn't be disturbed then." She'd done it deliberately, so that she'd hear him come in. She was waiting for him, waiting for this . . . scene.

"This is *my* house! I'll do what I like in it! And I will *not* be badgered in the middle of the night!"

"It is"—he glanced at the clock—"ten past eleven."

"If I say it's the middle of the night, it's the middle of the night!" She swept out. She's mad, he thought; she imagines she's God: let there be night . . . A moment later she reappeared and said, "Why don't you just quit?"

"I'm . . . not with you."

"Find somewhere else to live."

"I don't want to! I like it here. Very much."

"That's not true. You told Sarah you were unhappy living here."

"I did not. I said I was unhappy with the way you were behaving."

"Well, I'm giving you a month's notice."

He was staggered. "Why?"

"Because . . . because you're here too much! Under our feet all the time! We don't want a tenant any more. We like our privacy, Sarah and I . . . We don't have any privacy left and it's driving us crazy! You come into my room."

"What?"

"You come into my room."

"I've never been in there, except to ask you something. And I always knock on the door. I've never snooped round in your absence, if that's what you mean."

"I don't want you in there at any time! I don't want you knocking on the door asking questions!"

"You should have thought of all that before you told Aaron you were renting the room. You obviously aren't cut out to be a landlady."

"No. We've learned our lesson all right."

"What lesson?"

"We can't live very easily with someone whose standards are so different from ours."

Jack stared at her, then burst out laughing. "Do you mean *moral* standards? Harriet . . . I don't even have to stop for one *second* to ask myself which of us, by any decent code of ethics, is the more moral!"

"Oh yes." She nodded her head several times. "Our moralities are certainly different."

"I'm sure in the five months we've known each other, I've screwed with a lot more men than you have. But that is hardly the point."

A very disagreeable expression flitted across her face. "Will you please leave this house as soon as possible? If you find somewhere before the month is up I'll give you a refund on the rent."

"O.K. I'll go tomorrow."

She was taken aback. "You don't have to do that!"

"Tomorrow. The sooner the better."

Her voice rose to a shout. "Don't think you can appeal to Sarah about this! We've discussed it thoroughly and we're in total agreement!"

Early next morning he found Sarah in the kitchen eating cornflakes. "So it's a month's notice," he said.

"Sometimes it's better not to ask questions," she said, curtly. "Just accept the inevitable."

"I don't need to ask questions. Or do I? Yes. Just one. Are you happy with the role you've played in all this?"

She looked at him a moment, then said, quietly, "No."

"Pontius Pilate!"

"What do you mean?"

"You know very well what I mean."

He had an hour before he needed to drive to school, so he took the trail through the monastery grounds and up into the mountains for, he imagined, the last time. It was a damp, dewy morning, the air chill but windless. The monks' ungathered peaches lay rotting on the ground. October dust had become December mud, and water trickled in the stream-beds, splashed over boulders; it had been raining in earnest for three weeks now. There was a cheesy smell of fungus and rotting things mixed with the sharp pungency of eucalyptus and fennel. San José was smudgy, its edges blurred, its colors the dark green of evergreen mixed with grey. It's a dear, sad, sweet place, he said to himself; why do I love it so much? It's home, I guess: it's me. Of course it isn't the last time I shall see it. I'll be back.

He had phoned Richard after the fracas with Harriet, and was moving into his Castro apartment that evening. Fifty miles away.

I'm very naive, he said to himself, very naive indeed when you think about it. A Jamesian ingénu, the innocent abroad. I imagined you only had to tell a woman you were gay and you could launch into a nice, easy, uncomplicated relationship. How utterly ridiculous!

When he got back to the house, Harriet had left for the university. Sarah was busy reading her Bloomsbury book. They might never be alone together after this, so he decided to say what was on his mind.

"There was one reason, and one reason only," he said. "Am I right? I wouldn't sleep with her."

"Correct."

"I guess I shouldn't have wandered round the garden in swimming trunks, flaunting my muscles."

"Maybe."

"But I never brought anyone back for the night. Not once."

"What of it?"

"When she looks at a man, she does so as men look at men. At his crotch."

"Yes."

He smiled. "Tell her I've got a *huge* one."

"She's seen it already."

"Oh yes. I remember." He lit a cigarette.

"Not everyone in California's a kook," Sarah said. "Though in other states they think we all see our analyst every day, chat with our plants, eat raw seaweed, belong to satanist cults, and sit in hot tubs with fifty other people of both sexes drinking bottles of Almadén. Those who aren't flakes or fruits are nuts is the East Coast's opinion of us. But I do have to admit that Harriet can be fruit and flake *and* nut."

"Whereas you are fruit and flake. I'm just fruit, and there's nothing wrong with *that*. Why don't you leave her?"

She said, wearily, "What guarantee would I have that another relationship would be any better?" She then returned to her chapter on Lytton Strachey.

In the Fast Lane

No gay bar in San Francisco is exactly like any other: they all have quite sharply defined, distinct functions. If you want to meet a group of friends and talk, then the Café San Marcos is the obvious choice, for it has tables and chairs and little intimate corners like an English pub. The Elephant Walk, where Castro and 18th cross, is where you arrange to meet someone at the beginning of the evening; you go on from there to the End-up or the I-Beam discos, or even Trocadero Transfer. The Pendulum is the local black bar; Castro Station is for leather, and Badlands—Sadlands—is if you just want to be by yourself. The place for pick-ups, however, is the Midnight Sun. Which is presumably why it's the most popular bar in Castro: the only one that is so full by eleven o'clock on a Friday night that you have to queue up in the street and wait for a handful of satisfied customers to leave before you're allowed in.

It's a video bar. Everybody fixes one eye on the screen and more or less laughs at the entertainment, while the other eye furiously appraises the clientele. It isn't long before an arm is brushing against yours; or, when you turn your head slightly, a man is smiling at you, a knee touching the back of your leg.

You cannot come out of the Midnight Sun empty-handed. Unless you choose to, of course.

"You're a very attractive guy," said Wendell, this blond who'd been chatting me up for the last fifteen minutes. "Why else do you think I came and stood next to you?"

"You can actually see the trees for the forest?"

And we were kissing each other. Nice green eyes: green as gooseberries.

"First time I've been out in seven days," he said. "Is this a record?"

"Why's that?"

"Oh . . . a long story. Last Friday, about half past two in the morning, my room-mate and I were woken up by a knock on the door. There were two men standing there, blacks, with sawn-off shotguns. They'd come looking for drugs and money, and they weren't too happy when they didn't find a great deal of either."

"Je-sus! Did you call the police?"

"Oh, sure. . .look. . .I'll tell you more about it some other time, eh? A long story, as I said."

"We could go elsewhere," I said. "I don't particularly want to stay in this place all night."

"Where do you live?"

"Ah. . .that's the problem! Los Gatos. . .about fifty miles away."

"Oh. Well, I've certainly no intention of sleeping in my apartment right now; those two guys are sure to pay us a second visit. Mike—my room-mate—and I have been stopping all over town since last week. Anywhere except our own bedroom."

"Where do you live?"

"14th and Valencia."

"Why do you think they're likely to show up again? They did you over once; what's in it for them a second time?"

"*Us.* The evidence! If they rub us out, nobody can prove they did anything!"

I looked at him a moment in sheer disbelief. It was all quite unlike the home lives of our own dear queens in Exeter; but, I told myself, this *is* San Francisco: and even if I'd never seen much to suggest it was as violent a city as popular mythology would have it, I did know people who'd been mugged at one time or another. Every day some violent crime was reported in the papers, but I always assumed that the bad side of life happened in those parts of town I did not frequent. At two a.m. any city has no-go zones.

"Perhaps," Wendell said, "we can meet tomorrow. It seems like now just isn't possible."

"I'm going to a party in Oakland tomorrow at about seven. No reason why you shouldn't come too. . .Anyway, I hadn't intended to get back to Los Gatos afterwards. I thought I'd stop over with a friend who lives on 21st. Maybe we could both stay there."

He considered that, then said he'd call me in the afternoon. Meanwhile, he thought he'd be off to find his room-mate who was in a bar a few blocks away, looking as he was, for somewhere to spend the night.

I didn't think I'd hear from him again. What he really wanted was a bed till morning; why bother to get in touch with me tomorrow when there was obviously so much talent available who didn't live fifty miles away?

But he did call, and we arranged to meet at his office, which was in the Ferry Building, right down at the bottom end of Market Street. It was an odd time for anyone to be working, six o'clock on a Saturday evening. He was a free-lance copywriter, employed at the moment by a big firm of lawyers—he liked slaving over the weekends, he said, because the money was good, and he needed every cent he could lay his hands on, the first and most important item on his current list of objectives being to rent a new apartment as soon as possible.

He was not in the best of moods—edgy, hyperactive, and generally cross with life. Work had involved more than he'd bargained for, and he'd have to go in early Sunday morning to finish it off. He'd intended to get everything done, shower at the office, change, and come to Oakland with me, relaxed and ready for a pleasant evening. Now it wasn't possible. "Look. . .do you mind if I don't come to this party?" he said. "I just feel all tensed up. . .I won't know anybody there and I'll have to make polite conversation. . .I just want to wind down for an hour or so with a book."

"O.K.," I said. "It doesn't matter." John, who was giving the party, might be a little disappointed; when I called him earlier, he had been most intrigued to know who this guy was I wanted to bring. And I'd been looking forward to showing him off, I must admit. Well . . . it couldn't be helped.

"We can still meet later," Wendell said. "About eleven o'clock? Is that O.K.?"

"Yes. I'll have Aaron with me, my friend from 21st Street. He hates driving at night, particularly if he's been drinking. But he said when I called this afternoon that it was fine for both of us to stay there."

"Good. Good! In that case. . .come and get me from my apartment. Give two short rings. And yes. . .most important. . .before you leave Oakland call to tell me you're on your way."

The party was rather tedious, though there were friends I hadn't seen for a long time, whose company I usually enjoyed very much indeed: I couldn't wait, I suppose, to get Wendell's clothes off. He'd looked attractive enough in the Midnight Sun, and—surprisingly—even more so when I'd met him in his office. Surprisingly, because it goes without saying that a causal pick-up looks less attractive in the daytime than in the dim, sympathetic lighting of a bar at one o'clock in the morning. I liked his smile. The green eyes. And under the weary, adult face I could glimpse a nice young kid, a flaxen-haired Midwest innocent, who had ceased to exist not so long ago. Might even now be coaxed back into life. How old was he? Late twenties was my guess.

Tedious or not, there must have been something at the party to take my mind off Wendell, for I forgot to call him before Aaron and I left Oakland.

"I don't like it here!" Aaron wailed. "I don't like it here one little bit!" He locked both the car doors, and insisted I leave the engine running.

"If you're not back here in ten minutes," he said "I'm off home! Like a bat out of hell!"

"It's O.K." It could have been a lot worse: the neighborhood wasn't particularly rough or seedy; the houses weren't tumbledown, but it was sandwiched between two dubious areas—Mission, disreputable and Latino; and, in the opposite direction, a large public housing project mostly inhabited by poor blacks. "It's O.K.," I said again, and walked briskly up to Wendell's. Two short rings at the street-door as I'd been instructed: no answer. I tried a second time. No reply. What now?

A woman appeared, white, working class. Accompanied by a dog. "What do you want?" she asked. She was evidently just about to take the dog out for its evening stroll. I explained. "I don't know if he's in or not," she said. "Why don't you go on up and check it out?" All quite normal: it didn't seem like a block in which people were scared of their own shadows.

I rang at Wendell's door. Again, no answer, and I was just about to give up, when a voice called out nervously "Who is it?"

"Jack."

Much rattling of chains, bolts sliding, keys turning in locks. "Why on earth didn't you call from Oakland?" he gasped. "We'd have known who it was! We were convinced those black guys had come back to kill us! Why didn't you call?"

"I forgot."

Eventually I was standing in their living room. I had never before seen two grown men so terrified. Hands shaking, face muscles twitching, beads of sweat lining their foreheads. The adrenalin was racing so much that they couldn't stand still for a second, and their speech was almost totally incoherent.

Back at Aaron's house, several glasses of scotch were required to calm Wendell down; in no way was he ready to leap straight into bed with me. I began only now to grasp the full significance of what had happened to him a week ago, and why forgetting to ring from Oakland had caused him to be in such a panic. When the two blacks didn't find as much drugs and money as they'd hoped, they got quite nasty. Wendell and Mike were made to lie on the floor and were beaten about the head with the shotguns; the flat was then taken apart: chair covers ripped, crockery smashed, books and ornaments thrown all over the place.

"O.K.," one of the blacks eventually said to the other. "Shoot them both." He meant it, Wendell said; he certainly meant it. Why, I asked. What on earth good would it do?

"All witnesses to the crime would then be eliminated! I've told you that before."

Aaron, seeing my doubts, said "Believe him! This isn't London!"

"What happened then?" I asked.

"A noise—people on the next balcony; I'm not sure—frightened them and they ran off. But can you understand now? Why I'm sure they'll return? Why we've just got to find somewhere else to live? Why you should have called before you left Oakland?"

"Yes. I'm sorry."

He grinned, relaxing at last, and pushed my hair away from my forehead. "He's got a lot to learn about the big city, hasn't he!" he said to Aaron.

Aaron filled up our glasses. "We all had to."

"It's brutal, San Francisco. Yes, you can be a tourist and see only the Golden Gate and the cable cars and lots of nice men swanning up and down Castro, but really it's savage here, inhuman! I lived for five years in New York City and I much preferred it. At least I didn't get beaten up and robbed. Last week isn't the first time it's happened to me. I was mugged in broad daylight not far from the Golden Gate Park—this guy hit me with a gun, caused me a permanent neck injury. I still get a lot of pain from it. A *lot* of pain. Then I took someone I picked up for sex to my apartment and he tied me up and robbed me of everything I possessed. That was after we'd made love; I had to admit he was a fantastically good lay! He left me sixty cents so I could get the bus to work, and told me how to undo the knots . . . hmmmm . . . Life here is cheaper and more dangerous than New York. If I had any choice in the matter I'd be off to the East Coast tomorrow morning."

It wasn't the San Francisco I knew and loved. It didn't add up: there was something else I hadn't been told. "What sort of drugs were those blacks looking for?" I asked.

"Coke."

"Do you. . .do you sell it?"

He looked evasive. "Well. . .I have," he said. "From time to time. I need the money. . .Who doesn't! And Mike's unemployed."

The missing piece of the jigsaw, perhaps. Maybe Mike and Wendell hadn't paid their dues. A racket within a racket. Someone could have found out. Or, simply, the two blacks were the suppliers, and Wendell had been trying to doublecross them.

"How did they know you have coke in the apartment?" was my next question.

"Oh. . .they knew all right."

"Had you met them before?"

He did not answer that, just shrugged his shoulders.

"I'm going to bed," Aaron announced.

At last! And worth every moment of my impatience, though I was afraid I'd be limp: it was so late—two a.m.—and I'd been drinking since about seven o'clock. But, no problem. He was beautiful: hairy blond all over, suntanned; and he fucked superbly. God, I *needed* that!

"I feel guilty about Mike," he said. Mike had insisted he was O.K.— he'd taken a sleeping pill, and after we'd gone he was going to bolt, lock, chain and barricade the door. If he still couldn't sleep, he added, he'd get drugged up and wander the streets till morning.

"Nothing much we can do about it now."

"Ah. . .I guess he's O.K." Wendell was far from tired: he wanted more scotch, more cigarettes; making love was for him a stimulant. "I thought I might not get it hard," he said, grinning. "After all that psyching up. But it was fine."

"Yes. It was."

He stared at me and laughed: the first time I'd heard him laugh. "It takes a lot to slow me down!"

The pace of his life was certainly much quicker than my own. I didn't envy him that, not one bit. Nor the drugs. He had been on every one at some time or another, including acid. Really life in the

fast lane, this one: three a.m., and he was still talking. About his ex-
lover, another black. They had lived together for four years. "I loved
him," he said. "I loved him *totally*. I gave him everything, and in return
he just screwed around and gave me all the venereal diseases you can
think of. Now he's got Kaposi's sarcoma." Two years after the break-up,
he was still extremely bitter and angry. "I hate him!" he said. "I *hate* him!"

"Let's sleep, please! I'm so tired."

Wrapped round him, protecting him. Which I guess he needed, for
he talked all night in his dreams. Incoherent mumblings. Once he turned
over, twisted my left nipple, and shouted, "Are you satisfied? Eh? Are
you satisfied now?"

By seven the sun was so brilliant I couldn't even doze. So I sucked
his cock and he smiled sleepily: then he opened his eyes, his face lighting up with pleasure. This time I screwed *him*.

Aaron was discreetly padding about somewhere. "God! I have to
get to work!" Wendell exclaimed, and disappeared into the bathroom.

I found Aaron on the deck, dead-heading flowers. "Coffee? Help
yourself. What was he like?"

"Very good. Just what the doctor ordered."

"Hmmmm. Seems to be increasingly my role: bed and breakfast,
provider for other people. Well. . ."

"You do all right."

He concentrated on a particularly recalcitrant daisy. "Are you going
to see him again?"

"Nothing's been said on that particular subject. Yet."

"Well. . .if you want him, don't let him slip away home without
making another appointment."

"You like him, don't you?"

He glanced at the village spread out below us, and said, "he's cute.
And lively, and interesting. But. . ."

"But what?"

"I don't think I'd want to get mixed up with a guy who pushes drugs,
however cute."

I drove Wendell into San Francisco. Deserted Sunday morning Market

Street, peaceful September sunlight: impossible to imagine the brutality that had intruded into his existence. It was good to be in this city, I thought. It isn't cold, savage and nasty: not the image it presented to me. Which didn't mean I doubted the truth of what Wendell had discovered. Here you got what you deserved, perhaps, or what you wanted to find.

"I'd like to see you again," I said. No response. "Maybe. . .next weekend, if that's possible."

"I think I'll probably want to be out in the country next weekend. If I've got somewhere to live meanwhile."

"Come down to Los Gatos. I live right on the edge of the mountains. And there's a swimming pool in the garden." Silence. "O.K.," I muttered, more to myself than to him. "O.K., O.K." But why? We had got on fine: neither of us was tricking on a lover: sex was good enough to want it again: so?

So it was San Francisco, I guess. There was always some other cute little number round the corner, who might, perhaps, be just that half a per cent better than the guy you've got. Absurd waste of time, the whole business! Was the excitement of pursuit in the Midnight Sun really preferable to waking up with an old familiar face on the pillow beside you?

I went back to 21st Street and unloaded my complaints on to Aaron. He was still on the deck in his dressing gown, enjoying the weather and drinking his fourth cup of coffee. "Too bad it didn't work out," he said. "You made love twice? And talked for hours? And he doesn't want to see you again?" He shook his head. "He can do that sort of thing once too often. He'll wake up one of these days and suddenly there won't be anybody at all who wants to see *him* again. He isn't exactly a chicken."

"He liked you."

Aaron looked at me and frowned. "Did he say so?"

"Yes, just now in the car. Said he thought you were a very nice guy."

"Oh, I am. I am." He laughed. "If you go inside you'll find a slip of paper on the table. Tucked under the fruit bowl."

"What about it?"

"It's an address and a phone number."

14th Street. Wendell's.

"When did he give you this?"

"Last night. When you were in the bathroom."

"Don't do that!" Aaron had taken it from me and was slowly tearing it in half, then in quarters, and dropping the bits over the side of the deck.

"Not my type," he said, as the final piece fell into his neighbors' garden on Liberty Street.

"Balls. Of course he's your type!"

"So he's my type." We looked at each other and laughed: all those years of friendship. Better than any trick—however green the eyes, however much an innocent kid's face still showed through an adult's tiredness. "Have another cup of coffee," Aaron said. "And may you please catch syphilis from your night's exertions! May your prick rot and drop off where you stand!"

"That's not a very friendly thing to say!"

"It's what friends are *for*!"

The Gilded Youth of Los Gatos

Los Gatos. Middle class, moneyed, liberal; not a house that does not have two cars in excellent, often immaculate, condition, and a third or maybe even a fourth not so immaculate, indeed at times decrepit, the transport of teenage sons and daughters: the gilded youth of Los Gatos. Yes, gilded; for they too have money, from jobs not badly paid as they work their passage through school, or from the allowances of generous middle class parents whose generous incomes are derived from the silicon chip. And the skin of this youth is also gilded: sleek, silky and golden brown from the California sun, particularly the skin of the boys that fits so well on muscled arms and legs, on washboard stomachs and beautifully sculpted chests. Their hair is gold as ripe wheat, and their eyes are the brilliant blue of the sea.

Outside the 7-11 store, when they have nothing to do, the boys congregate, or they frequent the little park nearby and the lawn of the high school across the street; they chuck frisbees mindlessly at each other for hours, loll on the grass with their girls, or sit in their cars talking about girls, cars—and frisbees perhaps.

They are an aesthetic and sexual delight to watch.

So, when I run out of cigarettes, I walk to 7-11, although a pack of Marlboro there is ten cents more than at the tobacconist equidistant in the opposite direction, downtown across the freeway and the San Andreas. To look at the gilded young is worth a lot more than a dime.

Los Gatos is also a beautiful place. Its dignified houses, whose architecture has a hint of something chalet-style, Swiss, are discreetly embowered in shrubs and trees; its gardens are a profusion of scented blossoms in spring and summer. It nestles at the foot of the Santa Cruz Mountains whose slopes, clad in fir, soar majestically upward, giving the spectator a momentary illusion that he isn't in the United States but maybe in Central Europe, not too far from the Alps. But when his eye rests on the sun-drenched bodies catching frisbees, he knows for sure he is not in the Old World but is seeing a phenomenon that is pure California.

One Saturday in October I was walking back from 7-11 to the house where I live, smoking the first cigarette of the day. It was early, the overnight fog just beginning to lift. Fog swirled in the streets, though a mountain summit, gold in the dawn light, was visible through the dissolving cloud. It would be another hot, dry fall day. For the moment the temperature was chilly, yet there on the grass, wearing nothing but very short shorts, three of the gilded boys were throwing a frisbee. They were sufficiently good-looking to be a catch for anyone's bed, but one was a great deal more: a pearl of great price. Not yet twenty I'd guess, curly blond hair, fit, tanned, a slow, lazy, arrogant maleness in his movements. He would be my choice. I had, of course, no choice. All these gilded young men were heterosexual, or so I assumed. There was no way of finding out if they were not: they didn't patronize the gay bars and discos of Silicon Valley, nor did I see them on visits to the bathhouses or on weekends in Castro Street.

Across the lawns, outside the Civic Center, something very odd was happening — odd at any time of the day, but particularly so at twenty to eight in the morning. Around a grand piano, two men and two women in period costume were singing their heads off. Opera: I recognized it after a moment — the quartet from *Rigoletto*. The pianist was a young man in shorts, but decidedly not one of the gilded youth:

glasses, pale skin and an expression of deep intellectual and emotional concentration. They were being watched by a small group of early-morning walkers and their dogs; and the dogs—a German shepherd, a black labrador, a pekinese and a ferocious-looking doberman—were providing a vociferous accompaniment: yaps, yowls, howls, and from the doberman a sinister deep baying that seemed to be telling the singers "If only I could get off my leash, I'd sink a first class set of fangs into *you!*"

One expects eccentricities in California, but nothing I'd imagined had prepared me for this.

Even the frisbee throwers thought their game worth interrupting for a minute. "Hey, man, take a look at this!" said the pearl of great price.

"What is it, Kim?" asked the tallest of the three.

I made a mental note of that: Kim. Not a very jock sort of name, unless you're an Australian surfer or tennis star.

"Practicing for Carnival," said Kim.

They stood a few paces from me, sweat glistening on their incomparable chests and thighs. Kim produced a sweatband from his back pocket and fitted it round his blond locks: it made him even more desirable.

"C'm on," said the third gilded youth. "It's boring."

"Gee, look at that doberman!" said Kim, with a laugh. "It'll have a nervous breakdown!" He became aware of my interest: our eyes met, held for a moment longer than two strangers usually take to size each other up, then he turned back to the dogs and the singers, something slightly uneasy now in his face and the way he stood. The lazy arrogance had deserted him. It was a reaction similar to that of a man in a railway car who is bothered that another man sitting opposite him should look in his direction as if purposely rather than by accident; who regains his composure by crossing his legs or opening his newspaper, or suddenly finding an object of enormous importance out of the window on which to fix his eyes.

Kim couldn't do any of these things in the present situation. "Let's go," he said; and the three of them ran off to resume their frisbee game.

It was the absurd spectacle of those barking dogs rather than the absurd spectacle of the opera singers that dragged out of my memory myself at sixteen, John Coleman and the mummers' play, and presented a scene to my mind so vividly, with such total recall, that Los Gatos, the gilded youth, the mountains and the overnight fog for a few minutes completely disappeared.

When I was at school I used to belong to an organization called *Woodcraft*, a sort of Boy Scouts with a difference—no jingoism, no muscular Christianity (indeed no religious bias at all), and it was mixed. Its philosophy was conservationist, and though we sometimes went on sponsored walks to save endangered species like the orangutan, we were chiefly concerned with projects that would preserve the English countryside. We used to go camping on weekends, sing lots of songs, and amuse ourselves in a rather hearty, outdoor fashion. I enjoyed it, indeed approved of it—I still do. On one occasion we decided to perform a medieval mummers' play, the proceeds of which were given to some worthy cause; I forget what it was. This theatrical jamboree we put on twelve times in two days in the parking lots of various pubs in Devon and Cornwall; the first of these being outside the Royal Oak, Exeter.

I should add, at this point, that I strongly fancied one of the other Woodcraft boys, John Coleman, who was a year older than I, a very tall, good-looking, curly-haired blond jock—of course. We invariably repeat the same pattern in our desires and lusts, don't we? I wouldn't go so far as to say that I was head over heels in love with John—yet— but I desperately wanted to take his clothes off. I was still a virgin then: John, I'd decided, was the best example I knew of maleness to cure me of that.

The play was awful. I mean badly acted, under-rehearsed, and not taken seriously enough by any of those involved. This didn't matter too much, at least not in the Royal Oak performance, for the audience consisted of indulgent parents, aunts, uncles, and brothers and sisters who were very generous with fifty pence coins and pound notes when we passed the hat round afterwards. Unfortunately, almost all these families owned dogs, and the dogs, it being an open-air production, came along too. We had to shout our words at the tops of our voices as the barking was so furious and frenetic.

No really memorable disaster occurred until John (the hero) and I (the villain) had a sword-fight, in which I was supposed to stab him and he was supposed to fall to the ground, dead—though later in the scene he would be miraculously resurrected by some elderly saint who happened to be passing by at the time. John's mother was in the audience with her German shepherd, Sally, a friendly enough hound, but given to barking on the least provocation. Seeing John stabbed and collapsing melodramatically on to the gravel of the Royal Oak parking lot was more than Sally could stand. Breaking free of Mrs. Coleman's grip, she rushed towards us. She was obviously going to leap up at me, and, though I knew her sufficiently well to realize that she wouldn't tear my throat out, I considered it sensible to take no chances. I ran off, into the pub; Sally, instead of pursuing me, stopped by John, and sniffed and licked him, presumably to make sure he was still alive.

"Piss off, Sally," John said, loudly enough for everyone to hear. It wasn't a good example of medieval English, I thought. But the audience loved it; they cheered, clapped, and roared with laughter. The play's director threw his arms in the air and said, "My God! What next?"

The illusion of medieval England could not be restored now. Eventually John was brought back to life by the elderly saint, who was giggling so hysterically that the audience found this scene funny too.

When the play was over John and I went into the Royal Oak's toilets to pee and let out *our* stifled laughter—we were the only two involved in that performance who had kept straight faces. "My mum was so embarrassed!" he said. "She thinks she won't be able to look any of those people in the eye ever again!"

"They put more money in the hat as a result," I said. "They enjoyed themselves!"

"You're a peeping Tom." I was. I was staring at his cock. "It's more impressive when it's extended," he said.

"I'll bet it is. I wouldn't mind seeing that."

"Wouldn't you now!" He grinned, and adjusted his medieval tights. "There's food for thought!"

Many days passed with me not wondering *if* he'd let me, but *when*: I was sure it would happen. The thought filled my stomach with dancing butterflies. On a camping expedition in the forest two weeks later, the great event occurred. John went off for a walk, alone. I followed, and he knew I was following. When I caught up with him he was standing against a tree, half naked and wonderfully erect. Perhaps my memory plays me false, but as I recall, it was thick, upright and firm as a telegraph pole, a good eight inches in length. He unzipped my jeans, pulled my underwear down to my ankles, and lifted my tee shirt up to my armpits. Two pairs of hands then got greedily to work. For me, it was all too quick: I was so excited I couldn't control myself, and he was nowhere near ready. Typical of the age I was, I guess. At sixteen, seventeen, the drives of most young males are so strong that sexual activity takes only a few minutes and the sperm shoots great distances. Not so with John. He leaned against the tree in a lordly fashion, while my little hands frantically manipulated his cock. He took a cigarette out of his shirt pocket and lit it; as he smoked, he looked down in an almost disinterested manner at my efforts to bring him to orgasm.

Eventually he threw the butt away. "Why don't you suck me off?" he suggested. That quickened the process, and his pleasure in it; matters soon came to a splendid conclusion, John moaning and groaning loudly enough to wake the dead.

We returned to the camp separately. I lay in my tent and thought about it—the most marvelous experience of my life, I decided: I couldn't wait for it to happen again. But when I found John alone and asked for another session, he refused. "It's wrong," he said.

"Wrong? What's wrong with it?"

"You're supposed to do it with girls. I don't want to end up as a queer, a pouf. You can suit yourself."

It was like a vicious, unexpected slap in the face. I felt so hurt I couldn't answer, but walked off, hardly aware of which direction I was taking. I will never speak to him again, I said to myself.

But we did speak, and more than speak. He came to my tent later that evening, and said to follow him into the woods when no one else was looking. The same thing happened—gorgeous sex, then John full of anger and disgust. Yet our affair, if you can call it that, lasted the whole summer. He had nothing but contempt for me while I worshipped the ground he walked on. I was a poufter, he said, a freak, a kink, a.c.d.c., a faggot, a bum-boy, a bender, a brown-hat, while he — he only did it with me because none of the girls he knew would let him. Our last occasion was in his bedroom one afternoon when his mother was out. He fucked me. Though he was gentle pushing it in and he used a lubricant, it hurt like hell; I guess it always does the first time, and with a weapon that size. Despite the pain, however, I loved it.

His hatred was now total. "Get your clothes on, fairy, and get out!" were his first words after he'd come. His cock was still inside me.

He avoided me from then on as if I had an infectious disease. When I phoned him he replaced the receiver without saying a word. If he saw me in town he crossed to the other side of the road.

The quartet from *Rigoletto* came to a thunderous conclusion. It was well rendered, a neat parody of stereotypical opera singers; the tenor a little man with amazingly powerful lungs who stood on tip-toe to reach the high notes, the soprano much taller than he, vast in girth, with breasts of genuinely operatic size and shape. I never discovered the reason why they chose to practice outside the Los Gatos Civic Center at twenty to eight on a foggy morning.

The frisbee game was over, or perhaps had not resumed. Two of the gilded youth had disappeared, but Kim was standing under a tree, the frisbee in one hand, while the other intently adjusted the sweatband round his curly hair.

I strolled nonchalantly towards him, and, as I passed, I smiled.

He nodded, and said "Hi."

"What was all that about?" I asked. "The singing."

"Gee! A British accent! What are you doing in California?"

"I teach. At a school in San José."

"Really! Er. . .which way are you going?"

"I live up near the winery."

He grinned. "That's my direction too."

So!

We walked up the hill, exchanging bits of information: names, age, the fact that he was temporarily unemployed. Then we drifted into an uneasy silence. The boldness he'd shown when we first started to talk had trickled away; and the nervous, worried look with which he'd acknowledged my stare outside the Civic Center returned to his face. Would he like to come in for a cup of coffee, I asked.

"Aw. . .I dunno." He was very unsure of himself now. There was a long pause, but I wasn't going to break it. "O.K.," he said. "Just for five minutes." He glanced up and down the road, as if to make certain that no one had seen him.

It didn't take long to get him into bed. It was, you may certainly say, satisfactory; it couldn't be otherwise with such a beautiful body: the parts I couldn't see earlier because of his shorts were as generously endowed as the chest and arms and thighs. Another John Coleman. And, also like John, he didn't respond to caresses, hardly touched me, refused point blank to kiss, and turned his head away when I tried to kiss him. He simply wanted his cock sucked, then, when he was properly roused, to stick it up me and fuck. I thoroughly enjoyed doing exactly what he required.

Afterwards, as he lay beside me smoking a cigarette, he said, "That was my first time."

"Was it? I did wonder."

"I jacked off with other kids. . .when I was fourteen, fifteen."

"And since then?"

"I have a girlfriend." He looked at my bedside clock. "I must go soon; I'm meeting her in half an hour."

"Serious?"

He nodded. "I guess we'll soon be engaged. We plan to do that for Christmas."

"But you like men."

He shrugged his shoulders, drew on his cigarette, and gazed at the ceiling. "Yeah," he said. Then laughed. "All the time!" He turned his head and looked at me. "You've got a fantastic body." His cock was getting hard again.

"I keep in shape."

"I dunno," he said. "Is it a problem, or isn't it?"

"Sounds like a total mess to me. Do you like sex with your girlfriend?"

"Sure. It's great."

"But a man would be preferable?"

He nodded. "I don't want to be homo," he said. "I don't want to see myself like that. I want kids. . .and to keep my friends, the buddies I've grown up with. . .What would they think of me? I don't want to hurt my parents. . .I want to settle down and do the normal things."

"It's easier, is it?"

"I want to do the normal things," he repeated.

I thought again of John Coleman. When he left school, he went to the University of London and studied medicine, became — so I heard — a respectable and respected family doctor. Married a nice girl and bought a house in Romford. But the last news I had of him was that his marriage was breaking up. My informant didn't know the reasons; I didn't have to be told, however. I knew.

Kim was now fully erect; I wriggled down the bed and took it in my mouth. "Stop!" he whispered. "I have to meet Janice. Stop!"

This time he let me touch him — and kiss. The kisses were almost passionate. And, I felt, he released much more of himself as he screwed me. When he finally put his shorts back on, Janice had been waiting for some considerable time.

At the door, I said, "Are we going to see each other again?"

He looked evasive. "I dunno. I. . .well. . ."

"Where we met, where we first spoke by that tree. Tomorrow morning, seven-thirty."

He shook his head. "I doubt if I'll be there."

He was. With a volleyball, bouncing it up and down on one outstretched foot. No sign of the other two frisbee players, or the opera singers. Just early-morning walkers and the labrador, the German shepherd, the pekinese, and the doberman.

I hesitated, and stopped. For I had a sudden vision of the immediate future. This gilded youth and I would fall in love, have an intense, emotional affair. He was not going to marry Janice, nor have kids, nor continue to be loved by his parents and the jock buddies he'd grown up with, nor settle down and do all the normal things. I'd become his security, his survival kit, his world. And, like everyone else, I'd desert him too, because I would eventually, I guess, return to England. He'd drift away from Los Gatos to the streets of San Francisco, searching, looking for love. . .He would suffer.

I had no right to interfere so profoundly with another man's life.

So I stood there, trying to make up my mind, while he let the volley-ball drop to the ground, glanced at his watch, and looked anxiously in the direction from which he was expecting me to come.

Then, thinking of John Coleman, of what happened between us and what did not, I turned and began to walk slowly back home.

An Apple for the Preacher

At the baths that evening I saw an extremely cute Puerto Rican. Slender, fit, smooth; the skin drum-tight and gentle as silk to touch. Long legs, well developed muscles, a substantial thick length of uncut cock, the face a kid's face, unlined and innocent—large brown eyes, prominent cheekbones, and an urchin grin that revealed even white teeth. But he was not an adolescent: twenty-four, twenty-five, I guess; far from inexperienced in bathhouse games.

Everyone was on to him—moths and a candle. He liked all that attention: scores of fingers caressing and fondling, lips queuing up to suck, cocks jostling to be next up his arse. I don't know how many times he was fucked, or in whose mouth he decided to spurt—I couldn't get sufficiently near to see, let alone have the honor myself. I had to be content with stroking the skin of his shoulder blades.

When he had come, he couldn't leave the place quickly enough. He almost ran to his locker. I followed, and watched him dress: jeans, yellow tee-shirt, sneakers. Our eyes met in a long mutual stare. The look on his face was not friendly; it was . . . frightened. Very odd, I thought. In the closet? But the sex he had just indulged in was totally uninhibited.

He's one of the most beautiful men I've ever seen, I said to myself.

And he stayed in my mind's eye as I returned to the hunt and satisfied myself half an hour later on one of the beds, fucking a slim Chinese.

Next morning was the last Sunday in June—Gay Freedom Day. I went with Tom, Manuel and Adam to see the Parade: we stood, with thousands of others on Market, watching the Dykes on Bikes, the cohorts of moustachioed nuns, the drag queens, the floats, the gay organizations pass by. Gentle, warm summer weather, made all the more pleasant with can after can of beer and the gentle, warm friendliness of the crowds. Outside City Hall afterwards, we sat on the grass eating hot dogs, drinking more beer, and discussing tricks. Or the lack of tricks. And music, books, people, work. Etcetera. A vast concourse of gay men and women here, just enjoying the sun; rock music in the distance; talking with friends. Freedom.

Not far from where we were sitting was an obelisk that commemorates one of the city's last-century fathers; I can't remember who—nobody of great importance. A young man was climbing on it; I was vaguely aware of him out of the corner of my eye, but I took no notice, being more interested in Manuel's outraged account of Tom's disasters in their kitchen. It was, after all, a day when climbing on obelisks, shinnying up lampposts, or hurling oneself into a fountain was normal rather than a grotesque eccentricity.

Our attention was caught only when the people nearer than we were started to react very angrily to the guy on the obelisk. He was gesticulating with one hand, waving some leaflets with the other, and shouting. It was impossible to hear what he was saying; we weren't close enough. But the crowd was cat-calling and booing, and some people chucked empty beer cans at him. Unperturbed, he continued with his monologue. A girl and two large, hairy men climbed up after him. Gays are not violent: the two men could have stopped the speaker immediately, for they were twice his size—an arm-lock, a hand on his mouth, or throwing him into the mob would have been easy. But they merely snatched his leaflets and scattered them to the four winds, while the girl took off all her clothes. There she was, stark naked; not a pretty sight. She proceeded to waggle her enormous boobs very vigorously—up and down, round and round, side to side—an inch or two from the speaker, who took no notice whatsoever, but went on with his harangue as if she didn't exist.

The crowd loved this; a great burst of laughter was followed by thunderous applause.

"Is it some kind of cabaret?" I asked the man in front of me.

"Yeah, I guess you could call it that," he answered.

"It's some Moral Majority fascist," Tom said. "He's telling us AIDS is the curse of God for fucking with our own sex."

But I know this man, I suddenly realized, different though his clothes were; a dark suit instead of jeans and the yellow tee-shirt.

The entertainment was short-lived. A group of Parade officials arrived, clambered onto the obelisk, and forced him to stop. He was escorted firmly to ground level. The men who had snatched the leaflets followed, and the girl, rather unwillingly, got dressed. The crowd drifted away, looking for fun elsewhere. On the grass beside me was one of the leaflets. I picked it up: a manifesto from some obscure brand of puritanical Christianity I had never heard of, full of quotations from the Bible about the obscene behavior of Sodom and Gomorrah's inhabitants and the dreadful fate that befell them. TURN AND FLEE FROM THE WRATH TO COME shrieked its headline.

The Parade officials, having finished the incident without much trouble, were content to let the man go. I watched him as he walked about sadly, picking up the leaflets that were lying about everywhere. I felt sorry for him, and wondered if I was the only person whose feelings were ambivalent. Oh yes, he was insulting us; his thesis was ludicrous and his attitudes Neanderthal: but there is something brave—and pathetic—about anybody in a minority of one standing up for his beliefs in front of a hostile mob. Did he think of himself as a would-be martyr? One of the angels interfered with by the Sodomites? Despised like Jesus, rejected of men, a man of sorrows and acquainted with grief?

"Let's move," said Adam. "I need more alcohol."

"You go," I said. "I'm interested in our preacher."

"He's cute enough," Manuel observed. "Certainly cute enough. But you've as much likelihood of getting up his arsehole as he has of converting you into a Seventh-Day Adventist."

"You don't know the whole story."

"What story?"

"I saw him being fucked at the baths last night. I'm sure it's the same guy." The look on all three faces was one of the utmost astonishment. I laughed. "I'll see you this evening; I'll be in the Elephant Walk at half past seven."

I hurried away in pursuit of the little Puerto Rican, who was walking off in the direction of the Opera House.

It was not difficult to follow him, for he went at a reasonable pace and didn't look around. If he had met up with friends, got on a bus or driven away in a car, I would have been wasting my time; but I was lucky: he went home. He stopped by a tall Victorian house on Guerrero, and fished around in his pockets for the key. I sprinted, and caught up with him just as he was shutting the door.

"Excuse me," I said, panting. "Can I have a word with you?"

The same look of fear that I had noticed last night. "What about?" he asked.

"I'm very interested in what you were telling the crowd just now."

He recognized me; no doubt of it. He tried to slam the door, but I had my foot firmly in the way. I pushed it open—I was as big and hairy as the men on the obelisk.

"I could call the police," he said.

"Is that your usual answer when a man to whom you've been preaching wants to know more?"

He looked at me very suspiciously. "You'd better come in," he said.

His room was spartan—a table, a chair, an unmade bed, a few simple items of crockery. No ornaments, pictures, house plants; no books except a Bible. On the table was a typewriter, paper, and some small piles of leaflets. He sat on the bed, hunched and frightened—and just as vulnerably attractive as he had seemed yesterday. I tried to make myself comfortable in the chair.

"What I want to know," I said, "is why you indulged in wild, orgiastic sex at the bathhouse last night, then got up on that obelisk today to tell us all how wicked it is."

"What bathhouse?"

"Don't give me that junk! You know perfectly well I saw the whole thing."

He shrugged his shoulders, and did not speak for some time. "I'm an animal," he said, eventually. "Just as you are." His voice was low, barely above a whisper, and he gazed down at the floor. "There are times . . . try as one might . . . the animal is too strong."

"You appeared to me to be thoroughly enjoying yourself."

"Was I?" He looked up, almost imploring me to stop.

"You're beautiful."

Silence. Then, "You haven't come here to seek the Lord Jesus. You're from Satan to tempt me."

"And . . . do I tempt you?"

"I shall resist." A ghost of a smile hovered at the corners of his mouth.

So, I thought, he fancies me. "You imagine AIDS is the curse of God," I said. "I ought to beat the shit out of you for that! But I guess you'd enjoy it. And tell yourself it was the lot of the Christian martyr." He did not reply. "What would you do if I got on that bed, ripped off your clothes, and started to fuck you?"

He covered his face with his hands. "Don't!" he cried. "Don't talk in that way! You don't appreciate . . . how much I suffer!"

"I'm sorry," I said, more gently. "But you *were* enjoying yourself last night." He nodded. "Thus . . . having become a victim of temptation, you think you might as well go the whole hog. To sin in deed is no worse than to sin in thought. Yes? It sounds rather jesuitical. A Catholic argument."

He took his hands from his face. "I was a Catholic once," he said.

"So was I. A terrible load of baggage to carry through life, particularly if you're gay. When I got rid of it, I had no desire to crush myself under a quantity of even more useless baggage. I learned instead to enjoy my body . . . and the bodies of other men."

"Homosexuality," he said, "is evil, sterile, unfulfilling, and only causes misery. It has to be fought against."

"Did that crowd today look unfulfilled and miserable? Did it?"

He sighed. "No."

"I guess you mean your homosexuality has left *you* unfulfilled and miserable," I said. "One-night stands and bathhouse tricks instead of True Love. When True Love didn't materialize, you blamed your condition. And were a very suitable subject for whatever preacher or teacher warped your head."

"You should have been a preacher. You seem to have an answer for everything."

I grinned. "It's the Irish in me."

"I have . . . once or twice . . . thought God wouldn't look askance at two men who loved each other deeply . . . in a committed, caring relationship . . . "

"You'd allow yourself that?"

"What would be the result now if we undressed and screwed? After we'd come, you'd put on your clothes, leave, meet your friends in a bar and brag of the Puerto Rican trick who's the same guy who told them to abandon the ways of Satan. And that would be that."

"After we'd made love," I said, "I'd take you out to dinner. Then on to a disco. We'd go back to my apartment and make love again. We'd fall asleep, arms round each other, in my king-size bed. Tomorrow I'd fix breakfast, then we'd drive out into the country . . . look at the redwoods, maybe, or swim and lie on the beach. In the evening we'd go to this straight party I've been invited to. Make love and sleep together again. We'd talk . . . I'd discover your name, and where you come from; you'd tell me about your family, your interests, your work, your tricks, why and how you got stuck with this crackpot revivalist fire and brimstone. And you'd learn the details of my biography too. After that . . . well . . . we would just see what happened next. I can't outline more than the start."

We looked at each other a long while. "My name's Julian," he said.

I got up, went over to him, and pushed him slowly back on to the bed. He stretched out his arms, as in a crucifixion. I must do this carefully, by very gradual degrees, I told myself as I kissed him. Twenty minutes later I began to unbutton his shirt, though my cock was throbbing with almost irresistible impatience. After half an hour I had all his clothes off. He was hugely erect, juice spilling. My mouth explored the skin—face, arms, chest, legs—leaving till last the cock, now begging for it, crying out for it. My tongue, slowly licking its tip, caused his whole body to shake violently. It was more than an hour after we began when I pushed his legs up and very gently eased in my cock.

I didn't make the Elephant Walk at seven thirty—didn't get there at all that evening.

I often cursed the day we met; the twelve months that followed brought me more miseries than I'd ever experienced. I fell madly in love with him. I wanted to spend every minute of our lives together, in precisely that committed, caring relationship he'd said God would not look at askance. It was much against my better judgement: I'd been through all that when I was younger, and come out the other side wiser and happier I thought. No! The baggage—the garbage—he carried in his mind meant he would not move in with me. He refused to give up his evangelical work. He would get out of my bed, sweaty and trembling from a fantastic fuck, from both of us saying "I love you, I love you!" and go off to preach about the evils of gay sex. Sometimes he was so overcome with remorse he wouldn't see me for days on end, or he'd want punishment for the errors of the existence he was leading; and get me to handcuff him to the bed, make me beat his arse with a leather strap till he screamed with pain. I'm not at all averse to s.m., particularly the s. bit: more than once I've enjoyed flagellating a cute pair of buns. But that was with a stranger, someone for whom I had no respect, no feelings. Thrashing Julian's flesh till the welts appeared screwed me up almost as totally as he'd screwed himself up. There were times, however, when being with him was perfection: the week we spent in Hawaii, for instance, he left the garbage at home. It was a week of unalloyed happiness—laughter, warmth and sunlight: swimming, sunbathing, eating good meals, drinking, dancing, making love. "I want to spend my whole life with you!" I said.

"That would be so good!" he responded. "So good!"

But as soon as we returned to San Francisco he dragged that heavy, outsize cross from the rubbish bin of his mind and put it on his back again. In despair, I would bore Manuel, Tom and Adam to death with the tales of my joys and sorrows. They had never met Julian, and if it had not been for my obvious sincerity, they might well have thought I'd gone off my head and invented him—bizarre, Gothic, improbable. Julian always refused to have anything to do with them, or with the other parts of my gay life; it would be further temptation, he said. So we did not drink in gay bars, or stroll hand in hand on Castro, or go to parties and dinner parties given by my friends and acquaintances. Except for Manuel, Tom and Adam, I dropped out of gay life altogether. I missed it—another of that year's denials. All Julian would allow us was an evening at the I-Beam or the End-up discos, and that only in the rare moments when he was not torturing himself with guilt.

I would accept it, I told myself. Because things were certain to change. He couldn't possibly continue as he was: he was bound, in the end, to opt for one existence or the other. And that is what happened. He disappeared for a week—I don't know where, or why, or with whom, but when he returned, he tore up all his leaflets and threw them, together with his Bible, off the Golden Gate Bridge.

"I shall burn in hell for it," he said. "Of that I've no doubt. But the body's proved stronger than the soul."

"You could repent in . . . oh . . . fifty years' time."

"That's Catholic too. Lord, make me pure but not yet. St. Augustine. I don't think death bed conversions necessarily work."

"God is good. He'll have mercy on us."

As I eased in my cock, he said "And the Devil sure is attractive."

Next day was Gay Freedom Day again. Our first anniversary: a year had passed. I was not a bystander this time, nor Julian an inept preacher on a obelisk; we marched in the parade, hand in hand, holding a big placard he had painted: BORN-AGAIN ATHEISTS. That night, after

I had stroked the beautiful skin I could never tire of, licked the incomparable buns, sucked and roughly twisted the tits, played with the erect cock which was already spilling juice, put it in my mouth and my cock in his; after we had simply become two mouths giving two cocks exquisite, delirious sensations and our sperm had responded by shooting all over our tongues, I said: "The real start of our life together. I've never loved anyone as I love you."

He lit a cigarette, and thought for a while. "It's the end of our life together," he said.

"What?"

"This year disposing of my unnecessary baggage, as you call it: you've succeeded. You've made me throw it away, and I'm free now. But I don't love you for being the cause; I *hate* you. Satan can dress up in many costumes: he borrowed your body to win my soul. But I don't have to worship him too." He got out of bed and put on his clothes.

"Julian!" I grabbed hold of him; I wanted to hit him.

"Let me go," he said. "Please."

"But . . . what are you going to do?"

"As you said . . . learn to enjoy my body. And the bodies of other men."

"You've done that already!"

"I guess . . . I'll learn to enjoy anybody but you."

"I'll *kill* you!"

I didn't kill him, of course, but I was almost demented with grief. Tom, Manuel and Adam helped to nurse me through the depths of it, the pain, the tears, the sleepless nights. It was as if I were terminally ill. I left the city for a while, and found work in Los Angeles. I went for fourteen months without sex—I couldn't get an erection, or, if I did, it would flop before I was anywhere near orgasm. Time eventually grew a scab over the wounds, though it couldn't erase the scars; I could eat, sleep, have sex, even find other lovers—if that is what they were. Nothing was ever again on the same grand scale of passion and commitment.

I met Julian once years later. In a bathhouse—naturally. I'd already screwed three guys, so I watched him permit himself, somewhat halfheartedly, to be fucked by a hairy blond Scandinavian whose cock was of quite phenomenal dimensions.

We had a drink together, afterwards. "I hate you," I told him.

He was astonished. "Why?"

"Because you killed the love I had for you! You killed the capacity in me to love! That's the sin against the Holy Ghost!"

"The sin against the Holy Ghost?"

"Forgotten your Catholic theology? It's the ultimate. The ultimate sin!" He stared at me. In his eyes was the look of fear I knew so well. "We *all* have it within us to be devils as well as gods, Julian. Even you. I wasn't your Satan . . . but you turned out to be mine."

He quickly finished his drink and hurriedly left the bar.

I never saw him again.

At 21st Street

for Monty Rupe and Dick Brownlow

Aaron, alone on the sundeck of his house on 21st, drinking gin —
plenty of ice, tonic, a quarter of a lime — said to himself: twenty
years I've idled away in California. It was his usual hour for thinking
about existence, pondering on his problems (such as they were) and
coming to no conclusions. Oh yes, he'd enjoyed himself. Plenty of trips
to exotic places. Work — he was the lead guitar and singer in a group
call Gay Garbage, and the only musician in San Francisco's seventeen
gay traditional jazz bands who considered himself bisexual. Money:
he still had a lot, wisely invested, from the years when he was a famous
rock star, a teenage prodigy. Women, men: he couldn't complain about
lack of sex. And for the past fifteen years, he had been blessed — was
it really a blessing? — with having a lover, though Luke, at this moment,
was in England.

What was the point of it all? It was the way these cocktail hour
reflections usually ended: he'd dismiss the unsolved riddle by cooking
dinner, maybe going out to eat, watching TV. Or reading a book, go-

ing to a party. But I'm forty-five he said aloud, then—silently—well over half-way there. Maybe there isn't a point or purpose and the question is absurd. He was a handsome man, looked younger than he was except when the mirror chose to reveal the truth on mornings after. Fit, lean (thanks to his health club), suntanned. Eyes of the deepest blue. Long blond hair. He was still an eligible proposition, a divorced marketable commodity. He could still make a beginning.

The house, on stilts on a crazy hill, was exactly to his taste. It had taken years to get it just right, carpets, furniture, pictures, ornaments, plants, but now it was finished, complete. Nothing more to be done here. Even the deck looked perfect, shrubs and vivid flowers where humming birds sipped in the summer and swallows wheeled in the fall. The view was magnificent. Castro village immediately underneath, its ornate Victorians all shades of the rainbow like dolls' houses, and the church on Dolores with its spires of olive green and weathervanes of gold; beyond, the lego blocks and pyramids of downtown San Francisco; the grand sweep of the Bay to Berkeley and Oakland, and at the extreme left, the Golden Gate, at this hour in August always half-lost in fog. Sunset was often sheer magic. And after dark was no less beautiful—the city lights, the headlamps glittering on the Bridge, a milky way.

Fifteen years ago he'd written to Luke, who had an apartment in Santa Monica, and said, "You ought to live *here*."

"I don't like the climate of Sin City," Luke had answered. "Cold evenings and fog."

"What's Los Angeles?" Aaron said. "Freeways and smog."

They rarely met in those days though Luke had then been in California for some time. But they'd been writing to each other since Aaron had left England. Half a decade of correspondence, of small talk about good sex, bad sex, new starts and break-ups, mutual friends' doings and ill-doings, the vagaries of the weather and see you soon I hope. Real friendship had begun that night in England when they'd quarreled over Aaron's wife and fought a violent physical battle in estuary mud. Afterwards, they made love in the shower. Aaron hadn't done that with someone of his own sex since he was fourteen. Luke at the time was having an affair with a man, though he considered himself to be more heterosexual than gay. The episode in the shower had revealed more of their inner selves than they'd intended, and they liked what they saw. Some kind of unspoken promise was made; but Aaron was soon to depart for California.

A few weeks after he'd told Luke that L.A. was merely freeways and smog, he was on the deck with a glass of gin, thinking. The doorbell rang. Annoyed at having his reverie interrupted, he did not, for a moment, bother to move, but when it clamored again — several long insistent rings — he stood up, cursing whoever it was, and went to answer it.

"I've come," said Luke. "For good." He had an enormous rucksack, possessions sticking out of every pocket. He threw it down on the floor and sighed. "I could do with a drink!" He looked different — hair, moustache and beard quite short, almost smart. Greying a little. A Castro clone.

"What do you mean," Aaron asked, "you've come for good?" But he knew Luke was spelling out the promise made in the shower.

"To settle down," Luke said. "With you. It's time." Aaron looked blank. They were still in the doorway. "To share. To love and to make love." It sounded like a prepared speech.

"You've got to be joking!"

"I'm not."

"Then you're out of your tiny mind!"

"Are you going to fix me a drink?"

Aaron stared at him. His answer could be decisive one way or another. "Oh. . .yes. . .I suppose so," he said, and he smiled his most cat-like smile.

He had not been fucked before. Never thought of what it could be like: it was something totally outside his concerns. And he didn't want it now, for his memory wasn't exaggerating: Luke's cock was in width and length the largest he'd seen. Torture. He felt branded, scarred. An-

gry. Yet. . .maybe this is the purpose, he said. And wanted it again.
Within a month he was enjoying it so much he could not imagine
he'd ever found it excruciating.

To be absent was the real pain. When Luke was at work (his arrival
in San Francisco was because he'd got himself a column in the daily
paper) they phoned each other constantly. Together, they could not
stop touching. The bed became their bed, the house their house. For
the first time in his life Aaron knew he was doing something more
than playing games of love, of going through the motions of what
he had been conditioned to say and feel and think. And all he had
had to do in the end, he realized, was to take it when it was offered.

At forty-five they were still a couple, but—though there was no question of leaving each other—Aaron thought the purpose had gone. Luke
was fat and old: iron grey now and bald on top, in the leather he sometimes wore in the bars a parody of a Folsom clone. He frowned a
great deal, and was always sniffing poppers. Disgusting habit; the rooms
smelled of filthy socks. In bed he took ages to come, hours after Aaron
had lost interest or seen his own sperm white on his skin. *He* hadn't
grown old, he told himself, not sexually; even if his face was now lined
and the blondness of his hair was a secret between him and his hairdresser.
He still had all his energies. Luke had slowed down in every way: fell
asleep in front of the television, or just sat, silent and tired.

There had been quarrels of course, some of them quite savage. Aaron
had found that being fucked, however superbly, was not enough. He
went out looking for women, occasionally boys. Sometimes they shared
this third person, but when they did not, there was trouble. Luke rarely
wanted to hunt alone except at the baths and would get insanely jealous, hit Aaron in the face or smash things. Each time this happened
Aaron felt that one little bit of his love was killed. But what alternative
to staying together? None existed.

Increasingly over the years they had spent more time at parties and
dinner parties, and inviting their friends back. They drank more liquor
than in their youth, and were amazed at their ability not to get drunk,
at how they'd driven home without mishap. The social round, gay

or straight, had at one time been almost a nuisance, an interruption of the one thing they wanted, to be alone together, and when they had gone out, their conversation was a duet in praise of one another's physical beauty, fantastic performances in bed, goodness of character. Now, at these gatherings, they separated; it was a chance to talk to old friends, and if they mentioned each other it was "Well, of course, you know what he's *like*!" and "Naturally, he *would* decide to do that because he knows *I* don't want to!"

The view from the deck remained perfect, the summer flowers beautiful. The humming birds sipped, and the gin, the tonic and the ice always swirled satisfactorily in the glasses. It was often the only good time of the day, gazing at the sunset and swopping the small, dull details of the morning and afternoon hours they'd been apart. Even so, these occasions could be spoiled by petty arguments. Luke would moan about Aaron's cigarettes.

"Conversation twenty-nine," Aaron said. (He'd taken to deliberately annoying Luke by cataloguing the subjects they nagged each other about.)

"Well, maybe, but I've seen people die of lung cancer. It's not a pretty sight."

"They're my lungs."

"I have an interest in them."

"Stop worrying. You inherit everything when I go."

"Waste of money, too."

"*My* money."

"Oh. . .shut up. Do you want another gin?"

"Yes." Where's it gone, Aaron said to himself; where's it gone? I must do something! But what? A new lover? A trip to Palm Springs, Washington D.C., a cruise to Alaska? Go and live in San Diego? Emigrate to the West Indies? I've *got* to get away from him! But he'll still be in this house when I return. So. . .what *do* I do?

The day after he went Aaron wanted him back at once. It was only for a year—Luke had gone to England, a not-to-be-missed assignment with the BBC, a chat show; and it was a marvellous opportunity to have the break they both needed, to see friends, his brother, etcetera, etcetera. . .Why didn't Ron come too? He declined. He was looking forward to twelve months of liberty in San Francisco. A new start. . .perhaps it wouldn't happen at his age, but you never could tell. Not that he said that to Luke. Too many commitments, to Gay Garbage, to people he'd promised to see in New York City, and who would look after the house if they were both away for a year? He didn't fancy tenants wrecking everything they'd worked for. And there was nothing in England to interest him now.

Luke, aware of the real reasons, merely nodded.

But what do I do with this liberty now that I have it? Get drunk? Pick up a chicken on Castro and fuck it? Go to the baths? A fortnight in Hawaii? I can do all those things when he's here. So he took a vacation in the Baja and quite enjoyed it; the landscape was an undoubted novelty. But his fellow-travellers—rednecks scared out of their wits by the fluctuating value of the peso, the dollar's inability to open every door, the possibility of Mexican bandits and dysentery—wearied him to death. He didn't want to return to the empty house in San Francisco; so, neglecting Gay Garbage (there wasn't anything at the moment of great importance) and, spending more money than he felt he should, he went to the Galapagos Islands. Now here, at last, was something so different that his attention was held completely. He spent hours just watching the extraordinary birds and lizards and turtles, and the sea breaking over barren rocks; and said, somewhat surprised at himself, I'm happy. If only he could go on exploring new places for months on end, how quickly the time would pass! But he'd been everywhere at some time or another—Mount Fuji, the Nularbor Plain, the Taj Mahal, the snows of Kilimanjaro. There's always Poland or Lebanon, he thought, but he couldn't picture himself delirious with joy on the streets of Warsaw or Beirut.

So he went home, drank a lot of gin and limped round the house. In the mirror he could see capillaries turning his face into a little red map. Luke shouldn't have gone, he said; why did he? He knew quite well what I'd feel: that, of course, is why he went, the shit. Yes, I know I could have gone with him. How stupid I am! Even sex is better with him than the trade I still sometimes find on Castro. At least we talk afterwards, and he's there in the morning. He called Luke on the phone. "Please come back soon," he said.

"I'm here for a year," was the answer. "And I'm liking it."

"Liking what?"

"Nothing you'd raise objections to."

"You sound so far away."

"And you sound so near."

"What time is it?"

"Eight p.m.; we're in the middle of dinner."

"We?"

"Cheryl and Adam are in London. Why do you ask?"

"It's midday in San Francisco."

"And you have the whole afternoon and evening to get through."

"Yes."

"Ron, remember this. . ." A long silence. "I love you."

Another long silence. "I love you too."

In September, his nephew Stephen, who'd looked up his address in the phone book, arrived with his lover, a cute little snub-nosed blond of nineteen. They stayed for a month. It was a pleasant diversion; Aaron enjoyed himself doing all the tourist things with them—Fisherman's Wharf, Chinatown, Castro, the boat ride to Alcatraz, the Golden Gate, the view from Marin County. They went on the cable cars, and drove down to Monterey and Big Sur. Stephen and Bob had ostensibly come to Sin City to enjoy the fleshpots, but they only had eyes for each other. Stephen, a tough, dark-haired butch type, said with disarming candor, "I only want to fuck *him*. He's the ultimate turn-on." With the careless insensitivity of the young they hid nothing. Aaron, tidying up their room, was confronted with damp tissues, baby oil, KY, cock rings, dildos, stained sheets. They didn't learn this from my brother Peter, he said to himself. I last saw Stephen twenty years ago. He was seven then. Time. . .Rebecca must be grown up by now, too. And married?

Stephen had no idea. "We never see that side of the family," he said.

They didn't even bother to shut their bedroom door properly. Aaron, going to the loo at seven o'clock one morning, had a fleeting glimpse of beautiful male legs entwined and well-rounded buns banging away. As he peed he heard the cries of first-rate orgasms, on and on and *on*. . .He felt terribly jealous. Don't you ever think, he almost shouted out loud, that I might *care*? I, too, am still just a sexual a being! I fancy that boy like mad! You imagine, because I'm forty-five, I'm beyond sex, beyond feeling, beyond any consideration! Oh, how true it is that youth is wasted on the young!

They're at it two or three times a day. *Every* day. Just like I was.

One day they weren't: Bob came home by himself. "He's picked up some tart on Castro," he said. "He's welcome. See if it bothers me!" He burst into tears and fled to his room, slamming the door. Aaron decided to say nothing; he watched a film on television, then went to bed. He was woken at two a.m. by Bob slipping in beside him. "Fuck me," Bob whispered, and when Aaron did not stir, "Please."

Aaron propped himself on one elbow. "Are you sure you want this? Won't it lead to. . .complications?"

"Oh, get on with it, for Christ's sake!"

I'd like to do as I'm told, he said to himself, but can I? Suppose this is one of those occasions—it happens more often now with a stranger, the first time—that I can't get an erection? And if I do and once I'm in it goes soft? But maybe it was this young kid's beauty or his skill and enthusiasm; the only trouble Aaron had was holding himself back till Bob was near. Jesus, he thought as he came, it can still be as good as when you're seventeen!

"Hey, that was fine!" Bob said, admiringly.

Aaron roared with laughter. "What do you imagine? When you're over thirty it dries up? They wither and drop off or something?"

"That maybe you wouldn't get it hard. Or couldn't shoot."

"How do *you* know what it's like to be old?"

"You're not old. And you're not the first middle-aged man who's screwed me."

Aaron grunted. "Let's sleep now," he said, curling himself round the boy.

The following day when Stephen reappeared, the expected screaming match took place and the expected reconciliation. Aaron couldn't help but hear most of it.

"How could you *do* such a thing? My *uncle*! Dirty old man *pawing* you all over! It's *vile*!"

Aaron giggled.

"How could you go off with that silly little *queen*? Spotty-faced *mincing* adolescent! Probably given you *herpes*. What was she like in *bed*?"

Pause. "Not as enjoyable as you." A longer pause. "And Ron?"

"Mind your own business."

Oh, good for you, Aaron thought as he switched on the vacuum cleaner. You'll go far. Further than Stephen. Further than me.

When they left for England he felt lonely and lost once again.

Luke came home at Christmas. "But your year's only six months old," Aaron said.

"I missed you. It's God's truth, Ron: I cut the whole thing short for one reason—I can't be away from you and happy."

"I love you. Only you. Warts and sodding all." He threw his arms round Luke, kissed him, and wept real tears.

It was mild enough to drink cocktails on the deck. No brilliant summer flowers now, and much of the city was enveloped in fog, but the ice cubes clinked in the glasses as invitingly as ever, and the colored Victorians on Castro looked beautiful all year round. "Well. . .what have you been doing?" Luke asked.

"Nothing I haven't told you in letters or on the phone. You've heard about the Baja. The Galapagos. I'll show you the slides later; I'm quite pleased with them. Then there was a first-rate performance of *Turandot* at San Francisco Opera. Oh. . .I've read books, watched TV, kept house. Worked. And been to the usual parties, of course; seen the usual people. We're invited to Jack and Richard's tomorrow. Well, *I* am. . .I'll call them and say you're back."

"Good. I like their parties. Jack Crawley always does an excellent mousse."

"Same old mousse he's been doing for Christmas these past fifteen years," Aaron said.

"What about screwing?"

"While you've been away? Yes. And you?"

"Yes. Any good?"

"Let's say not important. One of them. . .was my nephew's lover."

"Your nephew's lover?" Luke raised an eyebrow. "Sounds like incest. Which nephew? You've got dozens; your family breeds like rabbits. I saw a selection of them when I was in England."

"My mother wanted to plant the earth with the seed of her sons. Curious ambition to have."

"Must have been Stephen. I heard he was over here, but I didn't know he was gay."

"Neither did I. More gin?"

"Yes, but not too much tonic. Ron. . .you're smoking too much."

"Conversation twenty-nine."

"I've seen people die of lung cancer. My mother did, and it wasn't a pretty sight."

"They're my lungs."

"I have an interest in them," they said together, and laughed.

"Waste of money too," Luke added.

"We've left a line out, haven't we?"

"It's not important."

"That wasn't it. Well, to continue. . .*my* money," Aaron said.

"Oh, shut up! At which point I say do you want another gin, but I can't as you're pouring them already."

"Yes, we're rusty, aren't we! The script hasn't been rehearsed for months."

"Talking of rehearsals, I'm in dire need of practice on your arse," Luke said. "I haven't seen real flesh since I last saw you."

"What about the others?"

"What others?"

"The sexy Brits."

"They're all wankers these days; don't know what's the matter with them. Country's going to the dogs."

"The matter is us," Aaron said. "We're too old for anyone to offer us much. Or perhaps you're not telling the whole truth? Anyway, the Americans are just as bad. They only want to suck cock."

"That's not true, either. Listen. . .take that gin indoors and get all your clothes off. Then lie face down on the bed, legs wide apart."

So this is what it is, he said later (not a scene of passion, not the athlete's performance he put on for Bob, but more affectionate, more tender than with anyone else, ever), not much perhaps but I'll buy it; it's O.K. He was still saying it over cocktails on the deck six weeks, six months, a year, years afterwards. It's the curling round me as I drift towards sleep, the day's odds and ends over the gin, the division of the domestic chores, the friends we feel really comfortable with, this house, the fact that he exists, that he's here now I reckon till death do us part. It's not much, but it's everything. How many others are as blessed as we?